WHAT IS
MEANT
TO BE

WHAT IS
MEANT
TO BE

WHAT IS MEANT TO BE

STEPHEN A. FORBES

ARCHWAY
PUBLISHING

Archway Publishing books may be ordered through booksellers or by contacting:

Archway Publishing
1663 Liberty Drive
Bloomington, IN 47403
www.archwaypublishing.com
844-669-3957

ISBN: 978-1-6657-6426-1 (sc)
ISBN: 978-1-6657-6427-8 (e)

Library of Congress Control Number: 2024916238

Print information available on the last page.

Archway Publishing rev. date: 08/17/2024

1

CHAPTER

All men, and women, that are born into this world, at a certain age or time in life, come to a point where they try to figure out, what will I do with this life I was given?

Some seem to know right away what they want to do with their life, while others just go with the cards that life has dealt them.

There are some people in the world whose purpose here seems to just be dormant, waiting to be brought out, and nurtured. Some go through life and never know what their purpose was for their time here on earth. It seems that some are put here to fail, so that through their failure and hard times, they inspire others to be all they can be and always move forward towards their goal.

Some start out on a path they believe to be theirs, just to end up never finding their way. Others end up finding a beautiful life they never could have imagined in what seems to be by accident. I believe all people have some kind of gift or reason to be here. In the end, no matter what one's plans are, It's God's plan for you that prevails. Good or bad, what is meant to be, is meant to be. My name is Gerald Strong and this is my story.

My mother, and father, Jennie and Dorrell, were born in Jamaica West Indies, and had come to England to get an Education.

My mother got into nursing school, and my father was into political science, and wanted to teach when he got his degree. He wanted to help structure young minds for the future of politics. Not just in England, but the world. The mechanics of politics he would say, we're the same everywhere.

Both parents were very civil rights minded people, and believed in equality, and fighting for one's rights. First by peace, and if that didn't work, by any means necessary. Both were avid readers of all things pertaining to balance of mind, and body, and peace among men. They were very compatible in that respect. They never complained or argued. Jennie, and Dorrell Strong had hopes, and dreams like everyone else, and plans, as to how they wanted to live their lives, and raise their children.

Then World War Two broke out.

After the war my parents plans changed, as did many people that fought, and made it through that terrible time in history. England, and France, as well as other countries and cities, had been bombed terribly, and my parents' frame of mind had hardened. The city they grew to love had been changed, and they felt they needed a change too. Both parents decided not to return to school. They moved to the United States, to New York City in the Bronx.

My father became a mailman, and my mother a housewife. Things didn't quite go the way they planned, but they were very happy none the less. They had two children, my brother Carl, and me, Gerald. War, and having two children, had changed my father's way of thinking a little towards violence. He now believed that most things had to be fought for physically, and believed every men, and women, should know how to protect themselves hand to hand. So I guess since things didn't go according to plan for my father, he decided to raise my brother and I like soldiers.

He had us taking martial arts lessons the minute we could walk. By the time I was Ten years old I was awesome in Martial Arts. I was like a gymnast too. I could back flip, and walk on my hands, and was very strong for my age. I could break boards, and I was fast with my feet, and hands.

When my brother and I came home from school, we trained, and read until we fell asleep. We read everything from Politics, to the Bible, having debates on everything we read. My father was right there in our faces at all times, giving up his leisure time for his family. We liked the attention too in a lot of ways even though we never went out to play like other children, and I never watched television.

My brother, and I never felt neglected in any way. My father had a sense of humor, and made the hard way we were being brought up and never doing things like other children, bearable. Plus we were both very good at what we were learning. My brother wasn't as good as me as far as flips and things, but he was so big and strong that he just overpowered his opponents. So we were quite feared in those circles at our age. We thought we were going to be some sort of fighter philosopher and teach both. Our course was set even for children so young, Or so I thought.

Then, when I was eleven years old, my mother and father decided they wanted to go to the big Christmas show at Radio City Music Hall that was located in the heart of Manhattan on 50th street on 5th avenue. This was one of the most beautiful parts of Manhattan.

With Rockefeller Plaza across the street, and the Ice Skating Rink. Saks Fifth Avenue, the famous department store along with Bloomingdales, as well as fine restaurants, and Central Park nine blocks north. Thousands of people walking in different directions going to their separate destinations, and all of them from all over the world. People came from everywhere in the world to try to make it in New York City. New York City was truly the Mecca of the world in Entertainment, Business, Fashion, and in every other category you could think of.

When we arrived at Radio City, the line to get in was around the block. It was December one of the coldest months of the year, the snow was seventeen inches high, and it was windy, and freezing. The wind was so strong and cold, when it hit you in the face, it stung your face and felt like you got burnt with a match. But once you got into the theater, you forgot all about the cold weather, the snow, and the long lines, and how long you waited to get in.

The magic of Radio City would take you over, and your imagination would begin to set in. Radio City Music Hall was one of the most beautiful theaters in the world. The theaters massive interior design just took you to another place in time. It had an eighteenth century look and feel to the place with its operatic design. The stage was gigantic, with red ruby curtains that were about fifty feet high. It had real wood work all over the a place that made it have a feeling of home yet still held the presence of a castle in a fairy tale. The unique thing about Radio City Music Hall was not just the magnificent look and feel of the place, but they had a live show before the movie came on.

First, a song and dance man came on, followed by fifty beautiful women called The Rockettes. The song and dance man wore a Top Hat and Tails like Fred Astaire, a well known song and dance man from the 40's,50's and 60's who was known for wearing a Top Hat and Tails. The Rockettes wore short skirts, and all had long pretty legs. They did this dance at the end of the show where all fifty of them raised their legs in air in unison. It was magnificent. Then the movie came on. It was The Ten Commandments starring Charlton Heston at the time, directed by the great Cecil B. Demille. He was known for making movies bigger than life itself in his time.

The movie, and the song dance man were so good, that it just touched something inside of me that seemed dormant. I believed that the actor was Moses himself. I wanted to pretend the same thing and be Moses, and make people believe for that little bit of time that I was really Moses.

The same way Mr. Heston made me feel with his great performance. I couldn't think of anything else. It was so inspiring, that I tried to part the Red Sea in the mirror when I got home. I put one of my father's robes on, and found a tree branch outside, and faced the mirror in my bedroom and said, "in God's name I part the sea". I meant it too. I was waiting for something to happen, but it didn't.

Right then, I knew I wanted to have the same power. To make people believe they could part a red sea because of a performance I made. I was struck for life, with a new direction. I wanted to be an entertainer. I had never really acted or sang that much but it ended up that I could hold a note, and liked to sing even more than acting, but because my father had me in his world, I didn't realize how good I could sing until I started belting out songs while walking to school. Singing in the shower.

My brother and mother had heard me, and said I sounded really good. It's funny how you can pick up words to songs without realizing it by hearing something over, and over again.

We would go to Church, and without knowing it I had picked up certain songs. This particular Sunday, the lead singer in the choir's voice got choked up, and she couldn't stop coughing. So I stood up, and started singing the words to the song. Everyone was surprised but joined in figuring God had something to do with this, and the whole church started praising The Lord.

My mother, father, and brother were crying with the Holy Spirit of Joy, and so were a lot of other members. The Pastor was saying Ha-la-lu-ya as I belted out the song. So many church members were crying and dropping to their knees and praising God. It was so powerful. The Holy Spirit took me over and through my voice engulfed the whole church with the Spirit of the Lord. I began to cry as I sang and felt the power of my voice do its work.

People talked about that day in Church to everyone they could. How the Lord took my voice, and made it a Holy Instrument. People liked what they heard and wanted more. I didn't realize that The music was in me waiting to be let go. I sang every chance I could after that. Little did I know that my being an entertainer would cause so much pain, and even death for friends, and loved ones in my future.

I performed in every school play that came up in public school. Since I won my father over with my singing, he let me perform as long as I didn't let my Martial Arts go. I practiced every mourning before school for an hour, and on weekends. People didn't know about that side of me and I kept it to myself. Everyone knew me as the kid with the voice.

People would come up to me and just point, and whisper, while others would come up to me and shake my hand and say, you're going to be a famous one day young man! I soaked up all the attention too. I was sensitive to all comments made about my singing.

Then I went to junior high school, and hooked up with this well known teacher Ms. Grossman. She was known for her perfectionism, and also for getting lot's of students into the schools they needed to go to, for acting, and music. She had ties everywhere. She was a little southern lady with a bad hip, and she walked with a limp. She must have been real fine looking when she was younger because she was pretty for her age, and had beautiful clear skin.

Her makeup was always flawless. She had a reputation for being a hard nose kind of music teacher, and was very good at what she did. I looked forward to being in her class.

I'll never forget the first day in her class. The class was an old time kind of classroom. With a big baby grand piano in the front of the classroom. As you walked further into the classroom, there were these chairs going upward in an oval shape at the rear end of the room that made the class look like a lecture hall instead of a music class. I remember the white paint on the walls. The paint was so extremely white. I always wondered how the walls stayed so white.

There were pictures of singers, and musicians on the wall that were not famous, and she was in the pictures with them, either playing the piano, or with a microphone singing. She always carried herself so properly, sitting in the chair with her posture straight, and chin up. A real southern bred lady.

When she addressed the class, she always stood to her feet, and when she talked, she always started the same way "Okay now children, I want everyone to stand when I call your name. If you're afraid of singing in public, if your shy in any way, well, you're about to get over that".

"Susan Spencer, your first."

The names were not in alphabetical order like we had hoped. Jerome Archie would have been first to sing if it was so, and we all would I would have been more at ease if he had sung first. He was Ms. Grossman's pet, and the lead tenor in the choir before I came.

He was also the class clown of the choir, even though he hid that from Ms. Grossman very well. If he went first, he would have eased the tension amongst us, because we all were a little nervous. He was a funny guy, he had lots of jokes. He was also shaped funny from head to toe. It was like he was put together with different body parts.

He had a really big head, and a little body. He was five feet two inches, and had a light brown complexion that was very dull looking. His clothes were always well cleaned, and ironed. He also had sneaky looking dark eyes that made him look like he was always up to something. He had really big teeth, and a lot of hair everywhere. Even on his arms, and knuckles. He gave out the perception that he was a really nice guy, but there was something that made you feel uneasy at times. His behavior was unstable.

He would be nice one moment, then distant to the point of a recluse. Like he was bipolar or something. He would snap at people when he was like this, and no one would talk to him at these times, which could happen at any moment. The only person that seemed to be able to get to him at all times was Susan Spencer.

Susan was one of those pretty blondes that should have been named Heather. Stacked in all the right places for a junior high school girl, and could really sing, but had to get over her shyness.

She seemed to like Archie, but because of her popularity, she didn't want to be seen with Archie because of the way he looked. Her friends would laugh at her, and she couldn't have that. So she only talked to Archie in music class, and if she did talk outside the class, she would let everyone think it was about music. She was so phoney.

She tried to come off like she was so confident in being herself, but when it came to her showing off that nice voice she had, she was so scared that she would shake. She had a bad temper too. She would have tantrums all the time, yelling at her friends in the cafeteria. She was fine, and talented, but she was certainly strange.

Well, Ms. Grossman was the perfect teacher to get her out of that. Susan was very popular, and she had an image to keep up, and didn't want to be shown up in front of the class.

At first when she was asked to sing, she was so scared that when she belted out the first notes, it came out sounding like a big screech. The class started to laugh, and Susan started to cry. Only Renee Burress and I didn't think that being embarrassed was funny. We knew that one incident like that could ruin someone's confidence for the rest of their lives. This was something that hadn't happened to me, but still I feared being laughed at also. Who didn't?

Instead of Ms Grossman consoling the girl, she got loud and angry and said, "Let's get something straight class. There will be no crying in my class.I don't like babies. That's why I never had children of my own."

"If you're not going to suck it up, and do what you have to do in my class to be the best you can be, you need to stand up right now, and leave."

"I won't hold it against you, I just don't want any babies around me."

"I have the best choir in New York City at the Junior High School level, and I intend to keep it like that".

"I'll not ruin my reputation by taking time out to pamper someone."

"Now Susan, try again."

Susan was so angry at the reaction that Ms Grossman had toward her that, she just belted out the tune with such authority in her voice, that all the class could do this time was applaud. We all stood up and applauded. This was the kind of thing that Ms. Grossman could do for her students. This made everyone that followed her, strong in their performance. No one wanted to let their teacher down, or go home. All of us in this class wanted to sing and be the best they could be. After a while, there were only two people left. Archie and me.

Archie was basically a nice kid, just sneaky as hell. Ms Grossman trusted him so much, and thought the world of him, but for some reason that he would never talk about, he hated her.

He would talk about her like a dog, and he would never explain why to anyone. He always kept his thoughts to himself about her. Despite how he felt about her, or how much he fooled around, he sure could sing.

When he sang, he had this high-pitched voice that would send out these beautiful notes with a power and energy that seemed so unbelievable for a guy his size and age.

Unfortunately, his voice didn't have that extra roundness that made you think that he would be anything but a choir singer, or background singer for a group. He didn't have that voice that could make him a star.

The song he had to sing was Chances Are by Johnny Mathis, and he sang it with perfection. The class stood up and gave him a standing ovation as he walked grinning back to his seat. He just knew he was good, and for that age and time, he was the best at that level until the new kid showed up. Me! Ms Grossman gave her class pet her stamp of approval with a nod of the head to him as he walked grinning from ear to ear back to his seat.

Now it was my turn.

The class quieted in anticipation. They all knew my reputation before

I came to the class. Some people had heard me sing already, and were waiting to see me up close while others just heard I was really good, and wanted to see if all the hype was true.

I stood up and straightened the bottom of my shirt. I took a real deep breath as I collected myself for the notes I had in my mind to sing. I was singing the Song Maria from the very popular movie, West Side Story.

At the time everyone knew the songs to this movie, so it had to be done right. Especially this song because this song started smooth and soft, and had to start out gently. As the song moves on, he had to be sung with authority. I knew I couldn't falter once in front of Ms Grossman the perfectionist.

So I started the song out easy and smooth, "the most beautiful sound I ever heard", "Maria."

"All the most beautiful sounds of the world in one single word,"

"Maria". "Maria", "Maria", "Maria", and I was off.

I had everyone in a trance. I could hear the quiet of the room because only my voice could be heard. When I finished everyone just stood up and applauded for what seemed like minutes. Even Archie was going crazy.

Ms Grossman just kept herself composed, but you could see she was affected by the beauty of the delivery I had made in the song.

She seemed strangely upset that I was so good. I guess she just didn't want anyone to know she was just as impressed as everyone else was. She looked up me and said,

"That was good Mr Strong", "there are just some spots you need to brush up on in your delivery".

"We will go over that in the future."

She really seemed disturbed by my performance instead of happy with it. It was such a strange feeling I was getting from her. I had never gotten such a dull, lifeless, reaction to my singing before in my life at that point.

The whole expression changed on her face from one studying her student, to hate.

Ms. Grossman could hardly hold herself up on her feet; she was so upset. She looked like she was ill all of a sudden. At the time I didn't understand what was going on, but I would certainly find out in the future what this was all about.

The girls in my class didn't have a problem with my performance. They thought I was fantastic and didn't waste any time in finding out if I had a girlfriend or not.

"Ladies I'm single at the moment, there is no time for playing around".

"Nothing can take my concentration away from my music."

"This is the time to get our direction straight, and get our heads together towards our goals in life."

"There will be a lot of time for steamy sex in the future." That really drove the women crazy.

I became a challenge to the girls from that point on. Who can make the new singer shy away from music and pay attention to them. I have to admit, this was a crowning moment in my life. I sucked up all the attention. All the attention of these women made me realize the kudo's that come with being a good entertainer. Now I wanted to be in this world even more.

All the women loved me, and all the guys wanted to be my friend so they could be around all the women. There were some guys that thought I was some kind of punk or something, and tried to pick on me. At that age, if you weren't into sports, and just sang and danced, the guys would pick on you, and call you a faggot, and many other names.

This guy named Butch Wilson heard his girl friend talk about me to her friends and decided to pick on me. He already was the biggest school bully and most kids were scared of him.

One day, someone showed me to him when I came to school, he and his buddies came over to pick at me. "Hey Gerald Strong!"

"Come here, I want to talk to you. He said", "you know who I am"?

"I said, no". Who are you"? "He replied", "I'm Butch Wilson." "I'm the top football, and basketball, and baseball player in the school and I'm the toughest kid in the school."

"I hear you sing real pretty". "Like a nice girl".

"I want you to sing me and my friends a song before we all go to class." "Let's see what you got."

I realized what he was trying to do. I looked at the situation. He had three friends with him. Did they all want to fight? I knew that if this Butch kid tried to hit me, that I had to take him down first. Then maybe the other kids would get scared and not jump in. I sure didn't want to hurt anyone. I just wanted to put him on the ground if he tried something.

"I said, look Butch," "I just want to get to class on time."

"He said, that's why we want you to hurry up and sing so we can all get there on time."

I began to walk away when he grabbed my shoulder. I spun around with a side kick to the stomach which knocked the air out of Butch.

The other kids just stood there while watching Butch gasp for air. I started talking then,

"I said, Look, if anyone else wants some, let's get this over so I can get to my class".

They all just looked at each other and said,

"no, no problem here". They helped Butch up, and everybody went to class.

That incident was like a shot fired around the world.

Everyone in the school was talking about that kick. People made the one kick into many punches that I had thrown along with kicks and twisting of arms, and all kinds of things that I had done to Butch. Now I was this big time fighter.

This really made me popular with the women now. The guys wanted lessons, and everything got out of hand for a while. But, no one messed with me, or anyone in the music department for the rest of the year. I never had to use my Martial Arts again in school for awhile.

Then the opportunity of a lifetime came when Ms. Grossman decided that the school play would be West Side Story, and that I would be Tony, the lead male in the play.

Ms. Grossman tried her best at every show she put on. She was very good at everything she did, but as you got to know her, you could see she was unfair at some thing's, and because of that, she didn't make the best decisions for the play.

She would put the wrong people in the wrong parts because of the attitude she had. Still, we did the show, and it went great. All the Junior High Schools in New York City were invited to see the play along with their parents. It was one of the best plays put on by a Junior High School in the history of New York City's school system.

Meantime, Archie continued to get on Ms. Grossman's last nerve as he constantly left notes on her desk, calling her "crippley". This made her crazy to the point where she had a class meeting and told everyone,

"When I find out who is calling me these names and disrupting my class", "I won't just take you to the principal's office".

"I will destroy you."

The threats did't stop Archie, he constantly teased her behind her back, and she never knew who it was that did it, and no one would tell either. This pissed her off to the point of sweat beads falling down her forehead from anger. The next day in class, she threatened everyone.

"Class when I catch this person",

"I'm telling you you're going to be really sorry!"

"Do I make myself clear?"

"Now class is dismissed".

Then when Archie got to where Ms. Grossman couldn't see him, he yelled out. "You'll be sorry Crippley!"

"Go hop away!" She was heated.'

She stared at me as she looked back.

I just looked back at her and thought to myself, why is this crazy women staring at me? I sure would find out soon enough. I just know her crazy ass wasn't blaming me for this childish shit. She was staring me right in my eyes too! Crazy ass lady!

This was the point where she started showing how mean she really was, and that she had been holding back a lot of anger towards people in general and was willing to use her students as hate's outlet. This teasing had put her over the edge. It had gotten to the point where every time she turned her back to walk away with her little limp, Archie would yell out,

"Crippley!" "You walk funny!"

All the class would laugh, not realizing that they were helping to spark this change in her attitude and unleash the real her because of their laughter. I know she thought it was me, but I just figured that the truth would come out one day, and she would see it wasn't me.

That day never came.

She became harder to deal with, but we had to continue in her class because it was our junior year. We had to hang in there and hope this problem between her and Archie would subside. I don't think any of us realized the severity of what was taking place. We were all still kids, and trying to find our way. How were we to know the deepness of pain that was being passed between Archie and Ms. Grossman. They both had deep secrets that was affecting the lives of students that had no idea of what was transpiring.

3
CHAPTER

My senior year had come. and it was already half way through the year.

It was time to get my song together for my tryout for the High School of Music and Art. It wasn't till January after the New Years and Christmas break but it was good to prepare early.

Music and Art was one of the best schools in the country for a person to get into music and acting for a living. This was the next move for my career in entertainment, and I was determined to make a statement with my voice.

Even though everyone was going crazy over my voice, I couldn't hear what everybody else heard. I knew I was on key, and that I was good, but that special sound that everyone said I had, I never could hear it.

You couldn't always hear what others heard. Just listen to yourself after you make a phone message. You sound different.

Through all that has happened, I still wasn't as confident about my singing as I was about my Martial Arts talent. I hadn't grown yet in confidence, but God had his reasons for not showing me full confidence in my singing at that time.

Meantime, Archie, and Susan, came back from summer break holding hands. They had fallen in love, and had become inseparable. No one knows where or how it happened. They were the first people I ran into as I entered the school. Archie was smiling from ear to ear.

He walked right up on me to make sure I saw him and Susan. She was really fine. She had filled out more and was looking really good.

No one knew how Archie pulled it off, but all the music class was very happy for him and her.

"Hey Steve, come here for a second."

"What song are you going to sing for your tryout"?

"I don't want to end up singing the same song and being the cause of your not getting into Music and Art because I sang it better."

"When they hear how good I sound, they might not want you."

Of course I fired back with, "they'll know the difference because I'm handsomer than you".

What Archie didn't know was that little remarks like that shook me up. I really didn't have the confidence in myself like I should, and every little comment from people really bothered me if the comment was not in my favor. I don't know where or when I developed this weakness. I didn't know who to blame for my not being confident in something I was so good at and loved. I didn't understand myself in this matter. I was looking for someone else to blame instead of myself.

The day had finally come for my song to be sung at Music and Art as part of my entrance exam and I sang the crap of the song. I sang Climb Every Mountain from the movie the Sound of Music. After I sang, everyone applauded for what seemed like an hour. The teachers that tested me asked if I could sing it again for some of the faculty. Some of the women started to cry in the audience. It was amazing! I knew I was In. Music and Art was the next phase of my career. I was going to be an entertainer, and this was the most important step towards my future, and I aced it!

CHAPTER 4

The end of the school year had come, and it was time for each student to find out what schools they had made, or didn't make. The schools were listed in a letter attached to each students report cards. Archie stopped everyone in the hallway after he found out, and was screaming at the top of his lungs, "I made it", "I made it." "I'm going to Art and Design!"

"I told you all I would make it!" "Look Steve, see!"

Susan did the same thing, and made the same school.

"I'm happy for both of you, now calm the hell down".

They said, "Open your envelope even though we know what yours says." They were right too. I was positive about where I was going. I just knew I was accepted. So I wasn't as excited as everyone else to see my results, in this I was confident.

With all the raving people had done up to this point over my voice, and acting, I just knew I was in. I knew I was heading to Music and Art first, then to Broadway, and a recording contract.

When I opened my letter, I was in shock! Something was really wrong. These fools are playing jokes with me and this is not the time to play. I looked at Archie and said,

"Stop playing, andGive me my real letter".

"This isn't funny." "I wouldn't play about this"!

Archie said, "I wouldn't play about something like that".

"Are you saying you didn't make it"?

I could see in his face that he wasn't playing. So I got a chill up my spine like you would never believe. I felt fear in my heart and my whole body. Like someone took my women from me or hurt someone in my family was confused. I felt disbelief. This couldn't be true. I felt empty and lost automatically. I didn't make it! First I said it real low a couple of times, then I yelled it out at the top of my lungs,

"I didn't make it!" Everyone got quiet around me. I just looked up in the air and said, "I'm going to the Principal's office and find out what the mistake was."

"Then I yelled, "Why Lord did they have to make a mistake with my paperwork"?

"This is not funny"!

I walked right into the principal's office and said, "Mr Murray they made a mistake with my paperwork can you find out what's going on, Please"

He just looked at me and said, "I've been expecting you."

"It's no mistake." "Someone didn't want you in Music and Art".

"Someone put bad bones on you."

"I could't find out who, but I knew this for days". "They said you were not talented enough",

"and that you were not the kind of student they were looking for to go to their school."

"You can't be talking about Gerald Strong." I told them.

"You're mixed up! He's the most talented kid I've ever seen". They assured me that there was no mistake.

"You are going to DeWitt Clinton High School.""

"It's an all boy school which is great academically and for sports."

"I just sat in his chair and cried". I couldn't believe I was in this nightmare. Right then and there I became cold and took the path my father chose for me.

5

CHAPTER

As time went by, the residue from my past still followed me around. When people saw me they would ask when I was going to start to perform again. I would tell anyone that asked that I had other interests now, but my reputation stayed with me for a while. I wanted to forget all about entertaining and concentrate on my scholastic career.

I ended up going to Dewitt Clinton and doing well. It was known for its sports, and I excelled in gymnastics because of my Martial Arts training. I grew in height to six foot two inches tall and became a good looking guy if I must say so myself. But, I kept to my studies through high school. I met a couple of girls and I lost my virginity, but nothing serious. My marks were very high in school and I had scholarships to anywhere I wanted to go. So I decided to go all the way to the other side of the country and go to U.C.L.A. in California. I didn't know anyone over there and this could be the perfect opportunity to start over. So I left my world behind to start.

6

CHAPTER

My first day on campus was the day I met the girl that would end up to be my wife. I was looking for the administration office and ran right into the most beautiful women I had ever seen to that point in my life. She had light brown skin with green eyes. She was about five foot ten inches tall with measurements of 40, 22, 34 and tight. Long thick brown hair down to her knees.

She was fine!

I asked directions to the office, and as I looked into her eyes I felt peace. She was so sweet. I just told her straight out, "At first I wanted directions to the administration office",

"but now I'm hoping that you would give me your phone number and let me take you to dinner, and a movie."

"What's your name?"

She answered me in the prettiest voice you ever heard and said, "Katherine, and yours"? I answered as smoothly as I could without seeming phony, or overly excited.

"Gerald" !

I wanted to know this woman. There was a connection, and I knew she felt it too.

It was funny how moving three thousand miles away from home

gave you confidence. We went out for about a month before she made love to me. We almost tore our clothes to shreds, getting them off.

She was so sexy it was mind boggling. Katherine was so beautiful, but when she was naked, wow! Even though she was right next to me in the bed, and my women, I couldn't take my eyes off of her.

I kept thinking, since I'm not a bad looking guy myself, if I hooked up with this woman, our children would have to be in a beauty contest at birth. Every thought I had about her was one of the futures with her in it. Plus, she was smart and had a great personality. She was the one.

I decided to not be passive and laid back in California. I displayed my Martial Arts openly by practicing in public with other artists. So I gained a reputation for fighting and being level headed about my talents. I got challenged many times and held my ground.

I was like a gunslinger. Every weekend someone new would show up to test their skills against this new guy from New York City. I was demonstrating kicks, and was doing back flips to get away from opponents.

I was breaking boards and bricks and showing some people the basics in how to protect themselves. Other Martial Artists tried me and all lost. Sometimes it got a little bloody, but all the Martial Artists that came, even though they may have been cocky, they still understood that these were not fights to the death or to maim someone.

All comers were professional.

My reputation grew fast and my name was all over the Martial Arts circle.

Meantime, Katherine and I started seeing each other everyday. I couldn't get enough of her.

Everyday seems like it was a new day with her. It seemed like she completed my words and thoughts before I even spoke a word. She was fascinated with my Martial Arts abilities along with my knowledge of things pertaining to our school work. So we studied together, and went everywhere together.

We would look at squirrels, play in the park, and just talk all day in our spare time. You know that if you go to a park to look at squirrels with someone, you are in love like crazy. We were inseparable. I talked with her about everything, and anything, but one thing.I never told her about my singing, or acting.

She loved music, and she loved movies, and I listened to everything with her, never singing a note, or tapping a beat with my hand. When we did go out, I showed no emotion to music or acting except to comment on whether I liked something or not. I would go and dance with her at parties, so she knew I could keep a beat, but that was the extent of my participation in music.

She asked me once, "do you know this song Gerald"? "Sing with me". I said

"no, I don't sing." I didn't say, I couldn't sing, I said, I don't sing, so I didn't lie.

After we graduated from college, I asked her to marry me. Both of us had degrees in Psychology, and I had a second degree in Physical Education so we figured we'd both teach for a living. We had wanted a big wedding, so we waited a year and a half, and saved until we were ready financially.

I entered a Martial Arts tournament to try and earn some extra money so I could take her to Hawaii for our honeymoon, and had made it to the championship match against the best in Los Angeles, Shue Chen. He was awesome.

I prepared my mind for the greatest challenge of my Martial Arts career up to date. He was extremely fast, but I had him beat with strength, and technique, or so I thought.

With that thought in mind, I concentrated on the task at hand, and that was to beat him down anyway I could, and win this competition.

The match was at the Forum in L.A. where all the basketball games were played, and where they had concerts. It was a gigantic arena. The crowd was packed with all kinds of famous people in movies, and sports, and others from all different fields. There were singers that I had seen it on T.V. my whole life. Even Frank Sinatra was there. It was a who's who of famous people.

When the match began, I got hit immediately by a front kick to the mid-section. He kicked me so fast I didn't see it coming. That got my attention and focus. I knew I was in for a tougher match than I had planned for.

His feet were faster than mine, but his hand speed was not equal to mine, so I threw a barrage of hand blows and low kicks to his legs. That kept him occupied while I looked for a flaw in his style. He kicked me with a kick to my side that almost dropped me. That jarred me real good but I recovered myself, and got started on his ass.

I realized that to get this guy I had to time one of those kicks he was hitting me with, and tax his ass with a good right hook, so I let him think I was hurt so I could get one good punch in.

I dropped my right guard down a little so he thought I was tired and that my side was hurt, opening up my defense. He went for it! When he came in I hit him with right uppercut and gave him a roundhouse to the stomach. He tried to kick me, but it was a weak kick because he was hurt.

When he kicked, I went low and swept him off his feet with a low sweep kick. When he dropped to the mat, I came down with my foot in his stomach.

Match Over! The crowd went crazy!

After the match, and I got my award, Katherine was jumping up and down with excitement. Some guys came running up to me to meet me, and they kept asking me, "Do you want to make some real money"?

"We really admired your style." "My Name is George Brent", "and his name is Roger Thomas".

"We represent BodyGuards Inc". "We get bodyguards for all the famous people in the U.S."

"We can have you guarding Eddie Murphy by next month and making 100,000 a year including expenses".

"Anywhere he goes, you go, all expenses paid".

"We have local work too if you don't want to leave the state."

"You can guard the stars just when they come to town".

"It's exciting work, and for someone like you, with your skills, it would be a perfect fit."

I didn't even have to think about it, I ran it by Katherine, and she was all for it.

So I agreed to take the job option where I stayed in the city so I could stay close to my woman. I was now in the entertainment business after all.

7

CHAPTER

A s time went on, I ended up guarding people like Stevie Wonder, the Rolling Stones, and the Jacksons and from time to time got that job with Eddie Murphy. I was wanted by all the stars that came into town.

Staying in the city to work ended up being the best move for me because I got to work with so many different stars, in all kinds of fields. It was a great job, and I lived a beautiful life.

Katherine, and I, had gotten married and we had had a big wedding. My mother, father, and my brother had come to the wedding as well as all the friends I met in California. Many celebrities showed up too, and Stevie Wonder sang You and I. It was a wedding to remember.

Katherine, and I, had two children. A boy and a girl. Louis and Maria. They were beautiful children. They never got in trouble. Went to school everyday, and as the years went by, they graduated from College.

Already I was forty-five years old, and I looked, and felt the same. God had been really good to me. I had been going to church through the years as much as I could. T.D. Jakes was my favorite Pasteur. He seemed to reach a part of me every time I heard him preach. The only problem was that he was in Texas. So I would try to fly down there as much as I could with the family.

I was able to save a lot of money threw the years, and I was at that age where I wanted to build up some equity, and retirement funds for my family just in case of an accident or something.

I heard about Tech companies getting ready to get off the ground, and a couple of other things too that sounded good. Other bodyguards I knew told me that it would be a good Idea to go to New York and listen to these people, to see what they were putting on the table as far as me investing..

There was a meeting being held at the Waldorf Astoria Hotel on Park Avenue in New York City next month, and I was told by friends to bring my checkbook with me. My contacts in the music industry said it would be in my best interest to go. I hadn't been back to New York since high school so maybe it was a good time to go and bring my family. I had never got to really enjoy my city as a youth. This seemed like a great time.

No one should remember me now. I had forgotten all about that world of being an entertainer and my past dreams. I never told anyone about my past, and in my new life, I put all thoughts of failure behind me.

8
CHAPTER

We went to New York in June. As the plane flew towards Kennedy Airport, you could see the New York City skyline on the approach. The World Trade Buildings, and The Empire State Building, and all of Wall Street standing tall. It was a magnificent sight to see. It put chills up your spine.

I was back in the city I loved so much as a young man. The theaters, and all the museums, and all the sites I grew up with were churning in my soul. I didn't even realize until that moment what I did to myself. I blocked out not just who I was all these years, and the city I loved, but a part of me that made me complete. I also gave up so easily my dreams after living a life of teaching others, and my own children to never give up. To always pursue your dreams. It was like at that moment, I came to realize I had lived a lie. I became a stranger to my city because of one let down. This made me remember my insecurities as a child. All this time had gone by, and I had never faced my past.

A man has many dreams in his life, some you fulfill, and some you don't. I had done well in life but this put a damper on my success. This was a mental lapse in my life that had to be faced. Tears started to come down my face as I felt the pain and foolishness of my past thinking. My daughter saw my tears and came and hugged me, not knowing what was really going on. She thought I was crying about seeing my city, if she only knew. She never asked me what I was crying about, and never told her mother and brother that I had been crying.

We decided to stay at the Waldorf even though it was six hundred dollars a day.

I figured I'd splurge on the family and show them a real good time. I payed for massages for everyone, and room service around the clock. Champagne and fine wines. I gave them three thousand dollars to shop. They went through that like water. The day of the meeting I sent them shopping. I decided to venture through the hotel and check out this famous place.

The Waldorf was one of the oldest hotels in the United States. It was elegant and only People with money stayed here. It was magnificent in design and size. It had a eighteenth century look, with a red carpet on the front steps leading upwards into the hotel. The movement of cars and people were tremendous. People were coming and going by the second. After you walked up the stairs on the red carpet, there was a huge entrance way leading to the lobby.

The workmanship on the inside of the hotel was of an eighteenth century look also like the front of the hotel except it had a mixture of modern day art on the walls. High ceilings, and beautiful woodwork everywhere that brought the look of old money to mind. Bellboys, and customers walking in all directions, people being shown to their rooms, while others where checking out the hotel. It was a grand hotel, and lived up to all that I heard about it as far as the stature and looks of the place.

I had been told to ask for the main ballroom in the hotel when I got there. Most hotels down in Manhattan had more than one ballroom, but the Waldorf had more than two, and they were gigantic. All could be construed to be the main ballroom, so I had to ask for directions. When I finally reached the main ballroom, at the front door there was a big, fat, baldheaded guy greeting everyone at the entrance. He was dressed well, nice suit, and tie, and new snake skin shoes. He just looked like he was visiting and wasn't part of the grand design of things, and He also looked familiar to me.

When he reached out his hand to greet me he said, "hey Gerald!
"What's up" ?
"How have you been"?
"Long time no see'.
"You still look the same as you did in JuniorHigh School".
I said, "You're familiar to me, but you have me at a disadvantage sir."
He said, "I'm Archie from Junior High. Remember me"?
I tried to play it off, but he looked terrible. I would have never
thought that was Archie, but said, "I knew that", but I wasn't sure.
He said,
"You're lying,I look terrible, but it's okay".
"I accept my looks". "I'm overweight and bald, but I thank you for
that Gerald."
I said, "It wasn't a total lie, I did think you were familiar".
"You've changed a little but we all have."
"Well Gerald, you really look in great shape."
"Still doing your Martial Arts"?
I answered, "how did you know about that "? I never told anybody
back then. He replied, "We all knew."
"You never said anything, and you never tried to be a bully, and
everyone loved you for it."
"That was part of what made you special besides your musical, and
acting ability". "Plus, that one incident you had with that kid Butch".
"We all had heard about that and never forgot it".
"Why do you think no one ever messed with you"?
"They were scared to get their ass kicked."
"What have you been doing all these years"? "I thought you'd be
famous by now'. I replied, "I am not into that stuff anymore."
"I am a bodyguard for very famous people". Archie said,"
"you call your talent, stuff"?
"You were the best I'd ever seen up to date. Are you crazy"?
"No one could hold a candle to you. What happened "?
I said, "thanks for the compliment Archie, but I couldn't have been
all that good if Music and Art didn't want me."

"I lost all interest in entertainment right then and there. I grew up, and realized I had to live in the real world, since then I've been very blessed."

"I married a beautiful woman, and have two beautiful children."

"I have a great job, and I'm in entertainment after all."

"I am the bodyguard for many famous stars".

"I made it, just not like I thought it would be, but I'm happy".

Like I said anyway, I couldn't have been that good the way everyone was raving about me back then, or Music and Art would have welcomed me with open arms. This is how things were meant to be. Archie looked at me with a look of shock, like someone just died or something. He said, "You don't know what happened back then?"

"You never found out why you didn't make it to Music and Art? That's why you've done this thing to yourself:?

"I looked him in his eyes and said, "what are you talking about Archie"?

He just continued talking saying, "that bitch won"!

"She succeeded in stopping another black man from being what they were supposed to be".

"I thought you were stronger than that."

I said to Archie, "What the fuck are you talking about"? Then he laid it on me.

"Ms Grossman stopped you from getting in".

"She was prejudiced against black people, and she also thought you were the one that was joking her back then".

"She thought you were the one leaving the notes, and without even knowing for sure, tried to destroy your life."

"She told her friends at Music and Art that you were a trouble maker, and that you were disruptive, and not well liked by your fellow students."

"She told them you had the kind of nastiness that didn't show up in your marks or talent".

"That you would be a major negative force for all that were around you, like you had been in her class".

"They bought it all, and turned you down."

"We all found out a year later, and they fired Ms. Grossman."

"We all thought that someone had contacted you, and let you know what happened."

"Now I really feel like crap, since it was me that did all those things to her."

"I didn't want to hurt anyone but her".

As he told me this, I had to just sit down and take all this in. I looked at Archie and said, "Why did you hate her so much? She loved you"!

He replied, "No! That was part of the game she was playing." Archie said, "I came to class early one day, and was getting supplies out of the supply room, when I heard her telling that real prejudice teacher Ms. Tracy, that she had me, and everyone in her class believing that she really cared about all of us equally".

She said, "All I want to do is cancel some of these little nigger's visa card to the good life".

"Every time I see a talented nigger, I try to hold them back and make sure they never get on the right road".

"My father would be proud of me if he knew just how many I've held back from being prosperous."

Ms. Tracy said, "You keep a count"?

Ms. Grossman said, "no, there have been so many that I can't keep count."

"All these little nigger's are good for is to keep me in a job".

"They say God never makes mistakes, but he did when he made them".

"They have no purpose like my Daddy used to say".

"They are so naive too".

"Take that boy Archie". "He loves me, and trust's me to no end."

"He is smart, and should be a scientist or something really important in life," "but he has no idea how smart he really is."

"He wants to be a singer so bad, that his dreams have clouded his reality."

"He will never be a singer, but as long as I let him believe he can be, he will pursue the wrong course in life, and will never be what he could have been".

"Someone that might have made a difference to his race".

"I told Archie that people like him never get anywhere in those fields where they use their brains to live because we lived in a world of prejudice."

"He fell for it, and changed his whole schedule around to be something he'll never be."

"They are so gullible".

Archie said, "Gerald when I heard her, it crushed me and my whole world. I just stayed in the room and cried until they left".

I said, "Why didn't you tell someone"?

"Why didn't you tell me"?

Others should have known this too. Archie looked at me with a somewhat discomforting stare and very sad postured grimace and said,

"No one would have believed me back then the way I played around all the time".

"That would have broke my spirit telling that story, and no one believing me, so I hoped that someone else would expose the bitch, and I would back them up, but it never happened that way."

"I'm sorry !" "I'm so sorry, but this is today, and that talent you've drowned still has to be in you".

"It's not too late."

You must already have connections to be heard".

"Give it a shot. What do you have to lose"?

In a very aggravated tone Gerald answered, "look Archie, thanks for the insight into the past, but I came here to get richer than I already am".

"I don't sing, or act anymore, and even though you've succeeded in making me feel like a real dummy for giving up on myself so easily, What's done is done"

"I have a great life, and I'm going back to it when I leave this meeting".

I don't depend on other people's opinion of me to guide me now".

"I'm grown" ! "I'm confident"! "I'm a husband, father, and damn good bodyguard".

Archie replied with, "I'm a scientist now Gerald". "I didn't listen to

her, and I went on to get my degree in Science, and then my Masters".
"I am trying to sell my ideas along with my partners."

"We are trying to start some companies dealing with computer
software".

"I hope you'll stay and listen to what we have to say."

"You might get rich like you expected sticking with us".

"We need investors to get our stuff off the ground".

So I listened to what Archie had to say, and I pulled out my checkbook, and invested in his company, but my thoughts were really on what
he had told me about my past. I have many questions now. I had to get
some kind of verification as to what he had told me. I knew right then
and there I had to see Ms. Grossman If she was still alive.

9

CHAPTER

The next day, I gave my wife, and children even more money to shop
because, I needed time to talk to Ms. Grossman. I got her address
from a friend in L. A. that had police contacts here in New York. It
wasn't hard to find her according to my friend. She retired after she got
fired, and always left a forwarding address for her mail. She was living
in a assisted living retirement home in Yonkers. I told my wife that I
still had some business that had to be taken care of, so I told them to
not expect to see me for the day. I rented a car, and took the drive up
to Yonkers.

It was easy to find Ms. Grossman, the place was about a mile from
the Major Dee-gan highway so that made it less difficult to find. The
place looked like it had been built during World War Two. The paint was
peeling, and the fence had a lot of rust on it. There was a security guard
that was at the desk with all the patients names, and room numbers.

I asked "do you have a Ms. Grossman here"?

He replied "wow! you're the first visitor she's ever got since I've been
here, room 206".

"Turn right, to the elevator, or you can take the stairs at that staircase
sign right there."

When I got to 206 I knocked on the door. I heard something

shuffling towards the door. When the door opened, it was an old lady with a bent spine. She walked with a walker, and her hair was completely gray in color.

She looked up at me and said "Well Gerald, I knew you would come one day, come in."

This was Ms. Grossman! Time sure treated her with cruelty. She was nothing like she was, not even a remnant of what she was. She looked terrible.

I said to her "You've been expecting me"?

"So it's true what you did all those years ago" ?

She looked me straight in the eyes and said, yes!

'And I enjoyed not seeing you on television or hearing about your singing career ".

"I did well with your destruction."

"I didn't expect you to be so easy, because your talent was so outstanding".

"But, as it turns out, you had less confidence in yourself than I could have ever imagined".

"Out of all the young little nigger boy and girls I ruined, you were my prize"."

You had the most talent I had ever seen in my life white or black or any color."

"My daddy would have been so proud of me for ruining you". It took everything in my being to not rip her head off her shoulders. I said to her as I looked her deep into her eyes.

"You evil bitch, you did't stop anything". "I am very successful and wealthy in many ways. She replied "yes, you well may be, but you're not famous"!

"You're up in age, and didn't do anything with that voice. You dumb nigger"!

I looked at her with so much pity, I couldn't feel sorry for myself. I just said "you evil bitch, there is a place for your ass in hell, with padlocks on it."

"No wonder you look so old, and decrepit".

"You look like the Hunchback Of Notre Dam". "Your hatred made you grow ugly inside, and out."

"God took care of you slowly, and has eternal damnation waiting for you when you die".

"I wouldn't trade places with you for all the tea in China, Witch!"

"You're alone, and you'll die alone".

She looked at me and cried. She started yelling at me as I left, "You'll never use that voice nigger, I did that!"

As I drove away, I didn't know what to feel, or think. I felt like a fool for stopping something I loved doing. I felt sorry for people like her, who were raised that way, to hate. I couldn't believe that this had happened to me. Why didn't I believe in myself, and all the people that said, I had what It took to make it? Ms. Grossman was right about one thing, I sure felt like a dumb idiot. Now, I wondered how things would have been if I had stuck to my dream.

10

CHAPTER

We returned to L.A. the next day. I couldn't tell anyone what I had been through, since no one knew what I had been through in the first place. I can tell you this, I felt so stupid about all that I had done to myself, and yet there was a comfort that I felt because of how good I had done in life up to this point. I had nothing to be regretful about because I was a success in my life, but now I was thinking, what if I tried to sing, and act at this age? Nah! I just laughed at the thought.

I had a job waiting for me to guard Eddie Murphy. He wanted to go out on the town. His regular bodyguard had to go to a funeral, and I had worked for him before many times so he called me, and one of my partners Bob Rains to stand in for him.

Bob was one of my best friends outside of family, and another Martial Arts expert.

We had done many jobs together through the years, and I trusted Bob with my life.

He was a proven warrior in battle. I had his back, and he had mine.

This night, Eddie wanted to go to some night clubs. This was always a pain in the ass when a big star wants to go out to a regular club. Everywhere Eddie goes, a very big crowd forms.

People loved Eddie. He was funny, and a good person, sometimes to a flaw. He usually listened to the advice of his bodyguards, but this night, Eddie wanted to get a drink from the bar himself instead of sending for it.

He wanted to go up to the bar himself, take the money out of his pocket himself, and buy a drink, and drink it at the bar. Big stars just don't do this, but this night he wanted to be a regular guy. This usually worked out to be a bad move!

As soon as Eddie pulled out his money to buy his drink, two big guys walked up to him and said, "Hey, Eddie". "Hey big star"!

You could see these guys had more than a couple of drinks and wanted to be assholes.

"Why don't you buy everybody in here a drink you cheap fuck"!

"We all know you can afford it."

"I'd like a long island iced tea, what about you Chuck"? Chuck was the other guy, and he was a huge dude. When Chuck started to speak, his speech was slurred to the point of sounding like another language, and he started drooling from the mouth.

He said "I don't like you Eddie." "You, or your movies."

"I don't like your dumb jokes."

"I especially don't like that stupid laugh you got."

"You sound like a damn horn on a boat."

With that note, Bob and I made our move in front of Eddie, and said to the two gentlemen, "Look, you both seem to be a little drunk right now, so Let's just move on so there won't be any trouble." Big Chuck said "We want some trouble, let's dance"

He swings this big fist towards my face. I just used his own force against him, and as he swung at me, I just pulled his fist towards me, and led him into the bar. Bob moved Eddie out of the way, and started working on the other guy. Chuck came again at me and I had to give an open palm to the nose, which caused him to bleed and not want to worry about fighting anymore. He was busy trying to catch his blood. Bob just knocked the other guy clean out with a right hook.

Then we grabbed Eddie, and took him back to the crib and made sure he was secure for the night in his home. Once we left Eddie, we went to get a bite to eat before we went our separate ways.

Bob was a character. He fought with a vengeance, and yet was a very kind and gentle person.

In his spare time, he would visit sick children in the hospitals. When we were not working out, he would be out trying to help someone. His skills in Martial Arts and boxing were great.

Not as good as mine, but enough to be very good at his job.

Sometimes I would let him win so his ego wouldn't be scarred.

Plus, I needed him to know I needed him if someone ever turned on me.

My Father taught me that you should never show all your cards anyway. Let some people think they were equal just in case you ever had to face them for real in battle. It would be to your advantage.

Bob was a single guy that went to church as much as he could when work didn't get in his way. He was about six feet tall, a good looking guy, and in great shape. I asked him some time ago why he wasn't married. He said because no women could put up with his weird ways.

On the outside he seemed like a good catch for some girl, but inside the house he was a neat freak, and said he was very demanding, and Religious. He expected women to serve him, and be submissive to the male species. He really seemed to believe that women should stay in the home pregnant.

He was in the dark ages as far as women, but in a fight, I wouldn't want anyone else by my side.

We had another partner named Albert Cain. He was really religious too. He was about the same height as Bob, and the same build. Six foot, and slender except, Albert had this strange beard, and big mustache that covered his whole face. You couldn't tell what he looked like under all that hair.

They were two very unusual men. You would never think these guys were bodyguards the way they felt about God and how they carried themselves outside of work. They were so much about peace and what was good for all people.

It was quite a contrast from bodyguard to their private ways, still regardless of that contrast Albert was another guy I trusted with my life, and in battle.

He was my boy, but he wasn't the kind of guy you wanted to be around that long. He was a great bodyguard but all he ever talked about was God. He had a way of making people shy away because he was over zealous.

He had one of those holy-er than thou attitudes. He would act like he never made a mistake in his life, and that he was perfect. He was a pain to be around sometimes.

I thought Christ had died for our sins because we could never be perfect, or so I thought. I believed in God, but I wasn't religious like them, still, they were my buddies, and I trusted them.

The next day, I met Bob and Albert at the gym to work out.

Bob asked "So how was your trip to New York"?

"Did you check out that business thing you were talking about"?

"Is it worth the investment"?

"I need some good investments in my life right now,"

Albert said. "So give us the 411 on the deal."

So I told them about everything, and they decided to invest also. They both knew I didn't spend my money carelessly, so they listened to most things I told them when it came to money.

I had made all of us good deals through years as far as our houses, and cars and things like that.

So they knew If I said go for it, then it must be a good deal. Albert would never invest in the stock market though, because he said that was gambling.

Albert said that because the soldiers gambled for the robe of Christ that made Gambling bad. I said, "Albert I though the chosen people threw lots that were like dice to decide who got what land between the 12 tribes of Israel."

He just looked at me and said, "That was different." "He made sure he gave his ten percent to the church."

The rest of his money went in the bank. As far as I was concerned, your money in the bank was a gamble. No matter how weird my friends seemed, they were both good people, and good friends were hard to find, especially when you basically beat people up for a living.

A few months had passed, and it was my birthday. I was going to be forty-six. My daughter, and son, wanted to throw a little bash at this bar for me. I had taken them there before when they reached drinking age.

They liked the place because it was like a family there. Everyone knew us, and they had this drink called a Singapore Sling, and everyone in my family loved it.

When we got to the bar the layout was fantastic. My wife had it catered, and there was all kinds of seafoods, and duck, and all the foods I liked, down to the dessert. Afterwards, Everyone was pretty high from the drinks at the bar.

The manager started inviting anyone to come up to the stage and sing.

They had a Karaoke machine, and a piano player that played anything you asked him to play. Everyone was so high that no one could hold a note. Then they got to me the Birthday boy.

They insisted I get up there and sing. Of course at first I said no way, but they pushed, and pushed, until I got up. I went up to the piano man and asked him did he Know A House Is Not A Home by Luther Van dross. My son got up and said, "now this should be funny"

My father has never even hummed a note let alone sing a whole song. My daughter said, "My Father doesn't know a whole song."

The bartender comes over to my wife and say's "What did you give him to get the old man up there"? I'v got to cut the alcohol content of these drink's yah think"?"

My daughter said to the bartender",

"Just make sure you record this for my video collection."

He said, "You better believe it."

Everyone got quiet, and was prepared to have a great big laugh on my account. The piano player started to play. I started out smooth and on key with every note as though I had sang this song originally. My voice was powerful.

When I sang this song, it was from the heart.

I even forgot where I was while I was singing.

When I finished the song, and opened my eyes,

Everyone was in shock. No one said anything. They all just sat there not saying a word.

My daughter got up on her feet and said "That was better than Luther Dad".

"I never would have thought in my life that you could sing like that".

"Was that my Dad"? "Was that my father that just sang that song?"

"Someone pinch me!" She was shouting as loud as she could. "Was that my father?"

Then everyone got up and started applauding, and screaming at the top of their lungs. The applause just kept coming.

My wife just sat there in shock. She didn't say anything. Everyone was quite stirred up about this new discovered talent they had just witnessed. The bartender poured a shot of whiskey for himself, and drank it down in one gulp, then started to applaud. Everyone was amazed.

On the way home, you could hear a pin drop. It was so quiet. My son was just shaking his head in disbelief. My daughter was just repeating out loud,

"My father can sing" over and over. As we pulled into the driveway, my wife broke her silence and said "I don't even know you."

"All these years you never sang a note, and now you sing like an angel."

"I mean, you don't just sing all right."

"You are like the best thing I've ever heard, and you're my husband".

"I mean, you never sang a note, ever!"

"Not even in the shower."

"I mean, how does a person do that"?

"How can you sing that well and never practice"?

"That's not normal!" "We listen to music in the car and you've never even hummed a note."

"I've never even seen you snap your fingers to a beat."

"Do you practice with some of those stars you guard in the studio?

"Do they know that you sing better than all of them"?

"I mean tell me something Gerald? "Does Stevie Wonder know that you sing better than him"?

"What kind of a person holds back talent like that from his family, friends, shit, the world. "?

Then she got out of the car and slammed the door behind her. My son just looked at me and said "you messed up dad!"

My daughter on the other hand was so happy. She started saying "We are going to be rich"!

12

CHAPTER

When I got in the house I called a family meeting. I told my family the whole story, and tried to make them understand that I was hurt, and a very insecure young man, with a confidence that was lacking in many aspects back then.

Still, they couldn't put the me of today with the one from the past. I seemed like two people to them now, and they were right. I had become much different man from that old Gerald. I just looked at my families faces, and did't know how I was going to get through this one, so I said "excuse me for a minute, I have to go to the bathroom."

When I got in the bathroom I just dropped to my knees and prayed to God.

"Please Lord, I know I haven't been a very active participant in the church, but you know my heart".

"I've tried to be a good, decent man my whole life, and tried to treat people they way I would like to have been treated".

"I love my family with all my heart."

"Please help them to understand the lack of faith I had in myself, as well as you, for not realizing the God Given talent you had bestowed upon me."

"I should have been stronger."

"Also Father, please help me along with what I'm about to do, cause I'm going to try to do what you put me here to do."

"I'm going to sing and act."

"Nothing will sway me from my purpose again, Father God. Nothing!"

"You've kept me in great shape through the years, and it felt so right up there on that stage".

"Please give me one more shot to use the talent that you had given me so long ago".

"I won't let you down Lord."

Meantime, my daughter had gotten on the phone and called the bartender at the bar I had sung at. She asked the owner "did you tape my father singing that song last night" ?

He replied "Yes, and I got the whole performance that your pops did, and I'm making copies."

"My place is going to be famous". My daughter replied, "Look, you scratch my back, and I'll scratch yours."

"I'm sending a copy to American Idol, and this will really put your place on the map."

He said "That's a great Idea!"

American Idol is the program where people sing for a chance at a big contract with a major music company. They have made many people famous in the music industry. The exposure was world wide. Even if you ended up in the top ten, you most likely would get a contract. My daughter didn't tell anyone about the tape and letter she wrote explaining my situation. Only the bartender knew about it. She sent Idol the video, and my story, and just waited.

They say it was the fastest response to a tape, and story in American Idol history. They responded two weeks after receiving the tape and letter.

It was now the first of June, and it was the day of my appointment to meet the judges. I had already knew them from the business I was in, and I actually worked for Paula Abdul before and she was one of the judges. Randy and Simon knew me from guarding other people and had considered hiring me many times.

They all didn't believe what they had saw and heard on the tape. They thought at first that it was some kind of joke someone was trying to pull on them.

So they wanted to see for themselves what the deal with me was. They wanted me to be at the studio in downtown L.A. by nine a.m. When I got to the studio the producers were interviewing the new candidates. They asked me to sit and wait for a moment. After about six or seven minutes, they rushed me up to the front of the line in the waiting room, and asked me to come into the studio. I was told I could sing anything I wanted without music.

So I belted out a couple of notes of the song, You And I by Stevie Wonder. Before I got halfway through the song they told me to stop singing. They said I had a great voice and didn't want me to sing another note until Paula, Simon, and Randy got there.

When the three judges got there and saw me, the first thing they said to me was "is this a joke Gerald," "because we don't have time for this".

"I replied", "Well listen for yourselves and find out".

"Randy said, you must really be bored with your job to come and try to sing".

"Your what, damn near fifty years old, and you think all of a sudden you can beat some of America's top singers".

"More power to you my brother".

Simon said, "My grandmother wanted to try out, and I didn't give her a shot, why should I give you one"? I just stood there and said, "are you all gonna hear me, or just get mad, cause I'm your age with a chance to be a rockstar."

They just laughed and said "let's get this over with",

"I'm sure we all have other things to do." "What are you going to sing"?

Paula says, "I want to hear the same Luther Vandross song he sang on the tape so we know it's him that sang it".

Randy and Simon agreed. "Sing A House Is Not A Home."

So the piano man started playing, and I started singing. I had them in shock. When I finished they just sat there speechless.

I said, "cat got you guys tongues"? They got very serious with me, and all just shook their heads. Randy was the first to tell me off.

He said "man are you retarded or something"?

"How could you keep that talent all these years to yourself"?

"That's just sick"!

Simon said, "If you can't explain this to us, I would have to agree with Randy".

"But I have a lot worse names for you than he does."

Paula just stared at me and said, "you are the best singer I ever heard."

"I don't think there is a story you can tell me to cover up holding back that kind of talent from the world."

"All the music you could have made".

"All the years of songs that could have been sung with that voice, gone".

"That's a shame"."

"No matter what happens from this point on, you'll never be able to make up for that time that is wasted".

"Who's gonna beat this guy, Randy asked"? It's not even fair."

"Yea, but the show will have viewers tuning in every night to hear the bodyguard with the new found voice Paula said".

"Were gonna be all over the newspapers",

"and every magazine in The world will be writing stories about this one",

"So let's get this show on the road".

I spent the rest of the afternoon telling them my story so that maybe they would understand more, but they still didn't get it.

They said I had no excuse. They were right.

Simon asked me, "please never tell that story on this show."

He said, "think of something better, and we'll run with that."

"Tell a story like, you lost your voice years ago, and it mysteriously comes back, that's all".

Randy and Paula agreed.

The news spread about my new found voice to my peers, clients, and associates. They all thought it was some kind of joke until they heard tapes. When clients asked me to work, they would want me to sing something. The word got out that I was the truth.

Well, the time came for me to go on American Idol, and as the time went on I easily made it to the finals. I was all over the television set, and in magazines like Paula said it would be, and much, much more. People were stopping me in the street's to get my autograph. I was already being offered contracts to sing and act.

Singers that I worked for in the past wanted me to sing on their albums.

Clothing lines wanted me to wear their clothes on the show. I was as the clean as the board of health on the show too. Even my wife and children were getting benefits from my success. My wife was as big as I was, at her job. She was bothered so much she had to take a leave of absence.

As the finals went on, my voice got even stronger, and people were voting for me from all over the world. Then it came down to me, and this young lady named Irene Taylor. She could blow too! She sang some Whitney Houston tunes just like Whitney, but in the end it was me that prevailed.

I won American Idol, and I was on my way for real! For the finally I sang Loves Light In Flight by Stevie Wonder. I brought the house down. When the judges spoke to me for their parting words as I was to go on my way to stardom, Paula started off with "You put chills up my spine every time you opened your mouth".

"Your already famous in my eyes, and I'll buy everything you record".
Next came Randy. "Yo Dog! you were awesome",
"but I think you already know that.You are the whole package."
Then Simon was next. He seemed to still have an attitude.
He said, "you know this really a shame, because you've denied the world of years of hearing your voice."
"I'm sorry"! "I think you should have won, no doubt",
"but every time I hear you on a record,
"I'm going to think how sad it was not to have had you singing all this time."
"All the other artist's that were alive that you could have sang with.""

"Songs written for you, and you alone, that perhaps no one would be able to ever sing better than you".

"Like Sinatra."

"You in some ways make me feel sad".

Paula and Randy said simultaneously, "shut up Simon"

Then Randy says, "don't listen to him dog. This is your time now".

Paula finished with,"This is the way things were meant to be"."Enjoy"!

13

CHAPTER

Back in Yonkers, Ms Grossman sat alone in her room in the dark. She was sitting thinking about all the people of color she helped to ruin, or slow up from getting where they wanted to go, when all of a sudden, someone grabbed her from behind, and wrapped her mouth with duct tape so she couldn't yell out.

The person then pulled out some piano wire out of the little bag he or she had around their waist. This person was of medium height and build, but Ms. Grossman couldn't tell if it was a man or woman because the attacker wore a mask. The attacker then proceeded to tie the piano wire around Ms. Grossman's hands and feet as tight as they could to the point of her bleeding around the wire's edge.

Once she was secure, the attacker started pronouncing sentence on Ms. Grossman.

"Ms. Grossman, you are accused of giving help to Satan, and his helpers on earth".

"Your punishment will be, to cleansed with fire, and may the piano wire be welded into your flesh,which was the tool of your trade for so many years."

"May God have mercy on your soul."

The person then reached in their waist bag, and pulled out lighter fluid.

The music teacher began to urinate on herself when she realized what was about to take place.

She tried to scream, but to no avail.

She prayed for help but it never came.

She tried to mumble at her accuser, and give him or her eye contact to remove the tape from around her mouth.

One last chance of mercy she thought, but once again to no avail.

She pleaded for mercy with her eyes.

She could see the person was enjoying her plea's, but still, she continued to beg.

This person was sure of the task at hand, and had all intentions of carrying it through.

Ms. Grossman's thoughts began to be mixed, as her mind raced from her past, and then back to the present situation. She thought of meaningless things as she began to shiver, and shake in what she knew were her final moments.

The attacker then poured the lighter fluid all over Ms. Grossman, and lit her aflame.

She tried to yell for her daddy as she burned alive, but the words never came as the fire engulfed her, and the duck tape melted into her face.

14

CHAPTER

I was a household name now. My picture was everywhere. Katherine and I started looking for a new house, and of course the children wanted their own cars. This was where the real fun came in, when I could spend money, and not really have to keep a close track on my spending habits., as long as I didn't go crazy.

We were doing good before, but now, the money was ridiculous. I became a millionaire right away. All kinds of companies were giving me things wherever I went, just to say I was in their establishment. They wanted me to say I used their products for publicity.

I mean they would pay me to say I slept in their bed, or use their toothpaste, then would pay me money, and give the product I was talking about for the service. It was amazing the attention I got, and how much money I saved being famous.

This new life was overwhelming. I was so blessed to have this happen late in life to because I don't think I would have handled the success as well if I was younger. I was so secure with myself at this age.

God knows what he is doing.

I ended up signing a contract with Sony Records. They had their hands in everything from Broadway, to motion pictures. I was going to make more money than I could spend in this life unless I was a total fool. Plus, my investment in Archie's company and the other stocks I bought were taking off.

I was rolling in dough. Now was the time to give back and help people who needed help. The contract with Sony was a lucrative contract with the freedom to pick and choose my destiny. It was all a singer and actor could dream of. Everything looked like it was going to be a storybook ending, but in each story, there are hard times, and unexpected twists and turns. I was getting ready to find out that mine were just beginning.

I started my first recording in Sony Studios in downtown L.A. and it was an experience from the get go. I was brought to a giant recording studio were all kinds of people were waiting for me. Somewhere their just to cater to all my needs, as well as songwriters to write songs just for me.

I had a guy named George Mason who was my gofer. He was a big guy, about six-five in height, about 220lbs. He was built like a linebacker. He knew everybody and everything that was going on around me. He was a serious guy to have around. He was there to run my errands and take care of anything I want, and I do mean anything.

I had messages waiting for me from entertainers wanting to collaborate with me on projects.

There were also a bunch of women all around that looked like Playboy Bunnies.

I didn't know anybody in the studio. All were strangers to me. All this chaos revolved around me, It was wild.

The writers asked me to sing a couple of notes to get an idea of my range, and the total sound of my voice so they could start on songs for me.

As soon as I started singing, the women surrounded me. Whenever I put the microphone down, they were right there. Sony gave me a voice teacher too. A very professional guy named Larry Roswell, and he had worked with many stars through the years, and I knew him.

Now I felt a little better seeing a familiar face. The first thing he said to me when he saw me was, "I should smack the shit out of you, but you'd probably fuck me up."

"You can't imagine how I felt the first time I heard that voice, and found out it was you behind it".

"I couldn't believe it".

He said, "I'm not trying to be nosey or anything but",

"I read some of the messages you had waiting for you before you came up,"

"and just as I expected",

"you have messages from people that don't believe your voice is legit".

"Some even say you made a deal with the devil himself".

"You're going to have to expect this from people."

"You've been in the business on this end".

"You know the crazy people out there."

He was right!

"I forgot about the threats from the outside world when you're famous."

I would probably have to hire bodyguards myself, for me, and my family. All of a sudden I needed to think.

"I asked Larry to excuse me, I told him I had to use the bathroom."

When I opened the door to the restroom, one of the girls ran up behind me and pushed me in.

I almost hurt her.

I said to her, "young lady, what are you doing here"?

"You know I am married."

"What do you think your doing"?

She was so fine, it was unbelievable. I had forgotten a woman could be so fine being married so long, and being so in love with my wife, I just never looked anymore. Right then I knew that this new fame was going to test my resolve.

She answered me in the sweetest, sexiest voice.

"I know you're married, but that voice of yours just turns me on to no end."

"If you need anything, I'll be here for you."

"No strings attached. If you just want to release yourself in me",

"or you just need me to go down on you, I will be there for you."

As she said that, she grabbed my penis in her hand.

The initial feeling felt so good, that I hesitated to take her hand off me. Her hand was so soft in my hand it made me weak.

She said, "all this chaos must be stressing you out."

"All you have to do is call on me." I removed her hand and said,

"I have a fine wife at home that can take care of that, thanks."

I had to run out of the bathroom. From that point on, I had my gofer George Mason checked the bathroom before I would go in for any women.

I knew I was weak, so no need to put myself in harm's way and get myself in trouble with some young girl.

This also made me realize that even though I was approaching forty seven, I was still a man who's libido was still in great working order, and might want one of those young girls in a weak moment. I had a lot of things to consider with this new found fame.

I had to keep my head on my shoulders.

The next day, the writers came up with a song that they wanted to run by me. The song sounded great! I couldn't believe people could come up with songs this good that quick. Once you get a song, you have to learn the song like it's a part of you, so you have to sing the song over, and over for a long time. Days! Weeks! Months! I never realized how much studio time you had to put in, in a day, week or month. I gained a new respect for singers.

Once you got the songs down pact, you had to hear yourself on a recording to make the sound right.

I got the songs down pretty fast according to the experts, and they were ready for me to record.

The whole studio was raving about my voice. The women were getting real dreamy eyed every time I belted out a note.

I couldn't keep them out of the studio because they were there with other people that worked for me, or around me. They would use guys or girls to get them in so they could try get to know the stars. This was my new world for a while, and I had to get used to it.

Meantime, my wife, and children, were reaping the benefits from my new career also. They were shopping all the time. I didn't see them too much anymore. I spent at least twenty hours a day in the studio.

As time went on, my family became distant. They were starting to hang out late from what I heard. Whenever I made it home, Katherine would tell me she was lonely..She was busy herself all the time with all kinds of people coming at her with deals because she was my wife, but as time went by, she couldn't handle all the attention that was coming her way from strangers. She wanted the same time with her family that she had before my fame.

The house always seemed empty, which made her stay out more.

She wasn't feeling as close to me anymore. She didn't like being at the studio with me because she would become jealous, and would disrupt the recordings. She we want me to stop what I was doing, and take her home, and that was out of the question with all the money that Sony was spending on studio time.

That's why in most cases they told me that having your spouse at recording sessions didn't always work, especially when your spouse was not an artist like yourself.

She lost track of the children, especially since they were actually grown, and rich. Both had brand new BMW's. They didn't have time for moms or me now.

They became rich, spoiled kids, and started doing the things that rich spoiled kids did for fun. They were trying to fit in with their new friends and in doing so, started on a road to hell.

My career was going North, and my family was heading South fast, and I didn't even know it because I was so busy all the time.

Some weeks had gone by, and I was to appear on David Letterman's show, and I already had a number one hit out. I got offers to appear as a special guest on many shows, and was looking at some movie scripts.

My family already was separated because of my fame. Before I knew it months had gone by.

I had an album out, and my first tour was being planned. Everyone wanted a piece of me like a really good apple pie. I made time for all engagements except my families company.

I had even forgotten about sex. Music was my lover now. My only contact with my wife and the children were on the phone. Katherine tried to fit in with the studio crowd from time to time but it never worked out. My fame didn't fit her at all.

She hated my recording family. She hated Sony's people that were around me, and she didn't ever like George or my voice teacher Larry.

I kept trying to tell her that as I got more control over my career that things would change and that we would all spend more time together, but I was fooling myself. The machine was running and you had to jump on board and change with it, or get lost in the shuffle.

I sang at halftime of the Super Bowl, basketball games, I was all over the air. Then I realized I had to settle down and get things right with me and my family.

I figured that prayer might help, and that's when I got an invitation to sing for Minister T.D. Jakes at Madison Square Garden.

This was my time to start giving something back to God, who helped me keep my health, and voice all these years. For this visit to Mr. Jakes, I insisted that my whole family clear their calendars so we all could be in church together.

My family and I met that Saturday before I was to sing for T.D. Jakes at our house, and had a big home cooked meal from the Mrs. At the dinner table we told each other all the things we had been going through. The children looked a little worn to me, especially my son Louis. He looked like he was not taking care of himself. Maria looked alright, but I didn't like the clothes.

She went to the house.

She looked tired, and wild at the same time. Even Katherine looked drawn out. I guess this was to be expected with all the things we have been going through. As soon as we finished talking, it was about time for the limo to pick us all up, and take us to the airport. We had to fly to New York, and be at Madison Square Garden by 9 o'clock. We all slept on the plane, and never opened our eyes at all, we were so tired.

As we approached the Garden, I felt a strange feeling coming over me. I felt some kind of connection that made me feel a feeling of comfort. Of peace. I also felt a foreboding feeling as far as my family's future solidity. I felt we would never be all together again in the same place.

Mr Jakes met us at the dressing room in the Garden that they had waiting for me, and I liked him right away.

He told me that I had a special anointing. and that I had purpose for having my gift be brought out so late in life., especially with all I have been through, was to bring people to Christ. Also, to let people know that it is never too late to go for your dreams.

Abraham, and Sarah, his wife, wanted a son of their own. Abraham was one hundred years old, and Sarah was seventy-five when The Lord told them they would have a son.

You never know God's plan, and that all have a seed planted in them. The seed stays a seed until it is nurtured. Once it is Nurtured, The seed becomes an orchard.

He said the seed was dormant in me until I let it out.

I felt his words within my heart. I had always liked him, and now that I met him, he was even a greater minister, and person of God than I could have imagined.

I sang Stand, by Donnie McClurkin, and something wonderful happened. I can only describe it as, The Spirit Of The Lord was in the church that morning. You could feel his presence all through your bones. Everyone in the audience was standing praising God. Men, and women, were crying in the aisles.

Then Mr. Jakes took over. He was a minister like no other. He had a unique style, and way about him that drew people to him. He started talking about the gifts from God that each one of us is given.

He said, "Each one of us has been given gifts when we came into the world".

"Each one of us is different".

"We have different DNA, because God made us all unique".

"Therefore our gifts are different also, which makes living on earth interesting".

"Allot of people can sing, but all sound different than one another, and we are all unique in our degree of talent".

"What is unfortunate is that, many of us go through life, and never find out what our gifts are, while others seem to know exactly what those gifts are".

"Some of us know Their gifts, and get caught up in life's struggles, and adversities, and because of the need to make money, never get the chance to go after their dreams."

"They don't realize that pursuing the gift, letting the gift you have come out, will bring you not just financial stability, but peace within and a content and happy life."

"Never getting to use their real talents, That is painful".

"To know, and feel, that you have a purpose here, and not get to pursue what you thought to be your destiny."

"This seems unfair, and very unfortunate."

"But what seems unfortunate to us, is part of Gods grand design for strengthening our resolve, and the resolve of those that look at your struggle from the outside and those that are close to you that see you from the inside."

"You know there is always someone watching you".

"Someone's always up in your business."

"Nosey family member, or a nosey neighbor".

"Well, they got inspired to move forward, because they watched you not reach your goals".

"They stood tall, and firm, and said", "I won't let what happened to him happen to me."

"They all developed Resolve".

"Some of those people help to keep you from reaching your goals if you don't stay on your course, steady, and true."

"You see, the meaning of resolve in the thesaurus is, being determined, making a decision, and the making up of one's mind to do something".

"It also means to solve something, or to make a resolution, a declaration, a ruling, a motion".

"All have been given free will to decide whether to try for the dream, or sit on your tail, and let circumstances stop you from reaching it".

"You see everyone is not here to be in the limelight".

"But all of us are here for a purpose".

"Even though you may not think you made it, believe me, you have".

"God has blessed you with life".

"All that are here today are alive". "You're all above ground".

"You're breathing God's air, and eating his food."

"No matter how good or bad things are, you are here for a reason".

"So since you're here on this earth thank God for that".

"A Lot of your friends are not here today".

"You want to join them"?

"I don't think so!

"I know that you have seen people in your life, that every step they take, seems to be the right step".

"They seem like anything they put their hands on works".

"They can't do no wrong."

"Well I tell you,everything ain't like it seems".

"Everyone has hard times, some might hide it better than others."

"Adversity is shared by all who live in the world".

"Some are here to make it, and some are not".

"We all learn something from the good and bad of life.

"So you must believe that all things are of God's grand design".

"He doesn't make mistakes".

"So when you see someone on TV, and they are ten years old, and a big movie producer was walking and said,"

"That boy is perfect for the part in my new movie".

"Don't say he was in the right place at the right time". "It was by design."

"When you see that ball player, he busted out that knee. Don't think that's it, it's time to step up the game, and push forward."

"You're still alive"!

"People are watching to see what you're gonna do".

Remember that it may seem that that person was in the right place at the right time, but you can't get nowhere unless you work at it".

"People never tell you the whole story."

"How they were homeless, parents left them on the doorstep when they were born"."

"They had to wash dishes, scrub floors". "No one just makes it without resolve."

"Things will not always go your way." "You have to stay the course."

"If something happens and you don't reach what you're aiming for, it's because that's not what you're here for".

"You might not make the mark because your other gifts are the ones you're supposed to be using in order to be an inspiration to someone else, so you can help them bring out their gifts."

"You must stay the course and never give up".

"This is the resolve I'm talking about."

"It's what you do, when things are not going your way".

"It's what you do when your back is against the wall."

"That's when you reach down in yourself, and realize, God gave you more than one gift.

"There is more than one gift in you".

"God had a back up plan for you." "That's why you're still here."

"That's why when trouble comes, you don't lay down, and die, and give up."

"Even when you became weak, you were an example to someone."

"If you're here today, you came through your weakness just fine."

"You're still here!

"Which example will you be "?

"If you got paralyzed, would you want people to see you crying, and complaining all the time, or would you want them to see you as an inspiration, and show yourself approved in God's sight."

"Being the positive force God intended you to be".

"To show yourself and others your strength."

"That's resolve"!

"I tell you, you're not using your real gift yet".

"Your real gift was the capacity to move on, no matter what!"

"Go forward, and be an example of greatness to someone else."

"What you thought was your loss, by you moving forward, is another persons gain, and strength, as well as yours."

"This may not seem as a comfort to you because, you wanted to be the one that was prospering in people's sight".

"You wanted to be the one that had that real handsome man, or pretty women for everyone to see."

"Everyone here wants to be all that because you're thinking in the flesh".

But Jesus said, "he has a mansion waiting for you.""

"Do you think he's holding that mansion for you because you were rich and famous"?

"He wants to see how you're going to be with what you were given to work with here."

"He doesn't care about worldly things".

"This is just a shell we live in here for a little while."

"That's why it doesn't last forever."

"There are no sinful people in God's house".

"There is no skin to get old, or botox to be bought".

"No stomach staples going on in Heaven".

"You are in perfection in the spirit".

"Everyone is equal." "You know they say, time is the fire in which we burn."

"Life is so short, and we leave so many things unfinished, that's why God had to give us more than one gift."

"He knew that you would pursue one path thinking that that was the path you were meant to go for. So when things went wrong or you failed at that direction, you would not give up and choose another direction."

"Finding out that the second direction was the one that would give you the most gratification."

"Slap three people and say, "I have more than one purpose."

"Who is smarter than him?"

"Your time here is set, But your spirit lives on. The spirit is "Eternal and is the drive that pushes you to do better in life."

"So if you don't have everything you think you should have had here on earth",

"and you don't look as good as you would have liked to look",

"or your health is not what you thought it should have been".

"Or some of you are not as endowed as you would have liked."

"That is a part of life, remember your real gifts are in heaven".

"Do your best on every level while you are here on earth."

"The Lord will reward you in the end."

"Remember that life is short, so don't waste your time feeling sorry for yourselves.""

"God don't like no chumps!"

"He wants soldiers in his army that fight."

"No matter what the situation, until there is no more breath in you. If you want to go back to school, go. It's not too late!"

"If you have something that's been gnawing at you for years to take care of, don't wait, go handle your business".

"You ladies want to go back, and show that man that left years ago, what they blew?"

"Same for you guys. You want to show that woman that treated you badly what they blew?"

"You thought they were a gift from God Himself when you met."

"Then they broke your heart; but later you met that real gift.

"You met that real gift because you kept going after they broke your heart."

"You kept fighting, and God awarded you your real gift that he had planned for you."

"You see, you knew this couldn't be all to life, so you kept moving on."

"Resolve!

"Say it", "Resolve!" "Can I get a witness in here today?"

"He was screaming at the top of lungs. Resolve! He said, "ya'll don't hear me" "I said Resolve!

The crowd was going wild with the Holy Spirit in the place. After the service, I brought my wife, and children, to meet Mr. Jakes. They seemed really inspired by him, and his message, at least that day. The family seemed to have a renewed relationship after that service. We started to see each other more often. I told Sony I had to see my family more, and they made it happen. When I went on the road, I tried to take my wife with me as much as possible. We started acting like we did when we first met. Making love all over the house, on the floor. Everywhere!

Then one night after making love, we were laying in the bed with all the lights out in the house talking, when we heard someone downstairs. I could hear my daughter's voice. She had company with her, so we didn't say anything at first. Then we heard arguing. Some guy was telling my daughter to stop being so greedy, and share the blow. Katherine, and I, decided to go downstairs and see who this guy was with our daughter, and see what was going on. To our surprise, our lovely daughter had a straw up her nose, sniffing a white powdery substance up her nose.

I went off on them verbally at first, then I grabbed the guy by the throat, and just held him still. I let him breath little breaths, as I explained that, "when I let go, you had better start telling me, that I'm not seeing my baby doing drugs, and this is a joke"

Then I realized, I'm not gonna be nice to this guy, so I threw him out of my house, literally. I told him, "if I ever see you around here again, I will break his arms".

Then I took all the drugs, and threw them out.

I sat down and said,

"How long?"

Maria said, "about a month, or a little less". "I just started partying a little."

Katherine smacked her right in the mouth. She fell down on the rug and started to cry, saying

"I don't have a habit, I just started." "It's only been on the weekends". "Why did you hit me?" "I don't deserve to be hit".

I told her My Daughter, "I've seen people in the business my whole career get destroyed from that crap." "Are you crazy?" "I raised you better than this."

My little girl looked into my eyes and said, "this is what these people out here do for fun".

"I was just trying to fit in."

Then my wife starts yelling at me saying, "this is all your fault!".

"Look at the kind of friends she has because you decided to wake up one day and become famous".

"This wouldn't have happened if we would have stayed in our other lives."

"We were happy!"

"There wasn't any problem that we couldn't handle together."

"You are the one that kept your talent a secret". "Why didn't you just leave it a secret!"

"Look what's happening to my family now?"

I fired back, "It's not my fault that you can't handle all this."

"I didn't teach my child to do drugs."

"She's doing that on her own".

"We had money before, and she didn't do this."

"There is nothing wrong with fame."

It's only wrong when you abuse it." "The decisions we make in life help determine our paths".

"You know I know". "Do you want to go the wrong way because of some drug?

Maria then said, "I'm not an addict Dad and Mom. I was just trying different things out."

I said, "that's how it starts for all who fall for drugs."

"Everyone says it starts out as fun, then it turns to a habit, and then destruction of life".

Maria then said what Katherine and I wanted to hear, "I won't do it any more." Then she tried to change the story. She said, "Anyway, what are you both doing here sneaking up on me?" "You both are never here anymore, why are you here now?"

Katherine said, "little girl, this is our house, we just let you stay here, and don't forget that!"

Maria shoots back with, "I'm grown mom, I can take care of myself".

"Louis has been the only one that's been in my corner since dad got famous."

"I'm a college graduate, and I can support myself."

Katherine says,"If that's true, maybe you should start working for a living", I said.

"Then you can see how hard it is to maintain your life". "You won't have room for drugs."

She said, "and I'll continue to see Peter".

"He's been there for me more than you two these past couple of months".

I said, "oh, so that's the asshole's name? "That's what you want, someone that condones your drug use.

She said, "you didn't even get to know him". "He's a good person".

I looked at my daughter as serious a look that I could muster up and said, "If you bring him around here again, I'l hurt him". Do you understand?"

Peter meantime, was listening at the door to see if Maria would be able to talk me out of hurting him the next time he came back, that"s when he felt himself lose consciousness.

When he woke up, he was at his apartment. tied with piano wire around his hands, and feet, to the point of bleeding.

Fear raced through his mind with the speed of light. He tried to speak, but could only make sounds because of the duct tape wrapped all around his mouth and jaw. He pleaded to his higher power for understanding in silence, but to no avail. His captor made his way in front of Peter so he could be seen.

Peter pleaded to his captor with his eyes for a chance to speak. He thought to himself that this must be a mistake because he had no enemies. "If I just had the chance to speak" he thought. Then his captor began to announce sentence on Peter.

"Peter, you have been pronounced guilty for the crime of dating the daughter of one of Satan's soldiers."

"You will be made an example so the bodyguard will take me serious, and renounce the deal he made with the evil one, to become famous".

"Do you have any last words before a sentence is carried out?

The captor then ripped the duct tape off of Peter let him talk, but Peter was so scared from the realization that he was going to die, that he couldn't utter a sound from fright. All he could do was shake.

He tried frantically to talk, but the words wouldn't come out. His mind was pleading for mercy, as his captor re-taped his mouth.

He then began to pour lighter fluid all over Peter. Then with no hesitation, he said, "may God have mercy on your soul", and lit the fluid. As the flames engulfed Peter's body, his last thoughts were, Why?

15

CHAPTER

I was getting ready to shoot my first movie in a starring role. I was very excited about it.

My love interest in the movie I was making was a tall, beautiful actress, that could entice Satan himself. She looked like Marilyn Monroe in the face, except she had pure chocolate skin that seemed to glow. She had the same body measurements as Marilyn Monroe 36,24,36.

There was a love scene where I had to kiss her. I didn't think it was going to be a big thing, and I was sure up to the task, or so I thought. When the time came to kiss her, as we drew closer to each other, I felt a warmth from her lovely breath that turned into a fire of passion.

The excitement I felt from her drew me in like a bad habit, and our lips hadn't even touched yet.

When our lips did meet, we both began to shake a little. As her body vibrated in my arms, she drooled a little saliva on my lips. It was like tasting a sweet nectar in my mouth. Immediately the muscle under my belt began to rise with the speed of a race car. I haven't felt anything like this for years with Katherine.

I pulled away from her, and looked into her eyes to see if the same response was showing on her face. It was! That's when her name really sunk into my mind, Jasmine Love.

I started repeating her name in my mind, over and over. As our eyes stayed fixed on each other, I knew I was in trouble. I tried to stay away from Jasmine as time went on, but one night there was a gathering of everyone on the set to practice the last scene before filming in full ward-rope. The last scene was to be shot at this hotel where the detective was to solve the big crime of the movie.

I found myself waiting for everyone to leave, and Jasmine was thinking the same way. It was about three in the morning when the last person left.

I was alone with this gorgeous woman, in a fantastic hotel, with a giant bed. She walked over to the bar in the room and said, "would you like a drink?" I immediately answered, "Yes, please!" I sure needed one.

While trying to concentrate on the drink she was making, she just started to speak so softly and said, "I know I'm wrong".

"Your Married, and happily from what they say, but something must be missing if we feel this passion for one another"."

"This connection is something that's been burning between my legs ever since that first day we touched."

"I've never felt like that in my whole life." I don't understand what I felt, but I know I want more."

Then she stopped what she was doing, and started towards me. My married mind said no, but lust said, "you'll never experience such passion again. Take her!"

She came towards me like she wasn't taking no for an answer.

She knew she had me. I felt the electricity as we drew near. We grabbed each other with the force of passion. We felt each other's breath, and bodies, dying for the touch of naked skin on one another.

We began to tear the clothes off from each other. I pulled her dress up around her head, and ripped her bra and panties off her. She ripped open my shirt, and began sucking on my nipples.

She slowly, and methodically traced the line down the middle of my stomach with her hand, until it reached the bulge between my legs. She ran her soft fingers around the pulsating veins of my love muscle ever so gently. That did it! We couldn't hold out any longer. I threw her on her back on the bed, and placed my tongue between her legs so I could get her lubricated, but she was already dripping wet, and ready for entry.

As I entered her, I thought I heard singing it felt so good. In what seemed like no time, and yet seemed like time stood still, the constant thrusting of my love muscle, along with the massaging of her gripping, hot inner walls, became a vibrating hold of lustful passion. After the first explosion, our passion got more intense as we made love over, and over, until we fell out on each other.

We stayed in the hotel for two days, not answering any phone calls, or knocks on the door. We talked very little, but when we did talk, we talked of what was happening between us. We knew it was just this time, here and now, and that this could never happen again. We enjoyed each other until the third day, then we parted.

As I approached my home, the closer I got, the guiltier I became. I had cheated on my wife for the first time in our marriage, and to make things worse, it was the most beautiful sex I had ever had in my life. I knew I would carry this one time thing to the grave, and keep it precious in my mind forever. As much as I loved my wife, I never had that kind of passion for her. I felt guilty, but not sorry for what I had done. I did realize that making love to my wife would never be the same again.

When I got inside my house, no one was home. I just laid my head down and went to sleep. When I woke up, I looked at the clock, and three hours had gone by. I rolled to my right side, and noticed an envelope on my bed. I don't see how I could have missed a big manilla envelope on my bed. It didn't have any name on it, or return address. I opened it, and pulled out the contents. My heart almost skipped a beat as the shock of the photos were absorbed into my mind.

There were photos of my wife, and children, in all kinds of different places. There were close up pictures of my son, and daughter are having sex with different people.

My wife at tupperware parties, and at meetings for charity.

There was a letter inside saying, that "no one can sing that good without practice for so many years unless they made a deal with the Evil One, Satan".

It said that my family will be the ones to pay unless I renounce this gift, and go back to my old job.

The letter said that, My family would pay first, then me. It said some have paid already for being associated with me, starting with the school teacher that started this so many years ago. Check to see if I'm lying.

I called the police right away. Reporters surrounded my house in a matter of minutes of the story getting leaked by someone.

Story headlines were, Mad Man Sneaks Into Home Of Idol Star With DeathThreat!

I was furious that the story leaked so fast. I had barely got my family together in one place to set up protection for them. A police detective named Robert Iturbi, told me he was in charge.

I asked,"are you people so unprofessional that you would jeopardize the well being of me, and my family, before we even know what's going on here?"

Iturbi turned slowly to me with his blue jumpsuit on, like I had interrupted his working on a car or something, and said to me, "Calm down Mr Strong, unfortunately these things happen when your famous like yourself." "It can't be helped". "Even police officers sell stories".

"I assure you, I will give them limited access to you, and your family, and your property, as soon as possible."

"I'll have my crew working with me, and they are loyal, I can assure you this won't happen again, unless we agree to leak something for our benefit only."

He seemed like a good detective that knew what he was doing. He was about six feet tall, and a clean cut looking kind of guy. He looked like he worked out a lot so I felt okay to a point. I still wanted my people around, so I ask Bob Rains, and Albert Cain to stick around for a while, and go through some evidence with me. There was no way in the world that I was not going to do the work by myself on this.

I had remembered that the day the girl followed me into the bathroom in the studio, Larry Roswell my voice teacher had told me that he had read my fan mail, and saw that someone said, I had made a deal with the Devil to get my voice back, so I figured I'd start there.

I was going to go to my staff, and find that letter if it wasn't thrown away. Also, with Bob, and Albert around, that was added protection for my family.

I could take care of myself, and this person knew that. He sure could have killed me in my sleep, I wondered why he didn't just end this right then and there, and solve his problem with me.

That bewildered me. I would never be so vulnerable again. I'll sleep light for now on, and get a trained dog that will stay with me, and my family when we are at home. One that won't bark on entry, only when they try to leave.

When Bob, and Albert showed up, they were steaming mad at the thought that someone had the nerve to threaten me, and mine. I had filled them in on the phone when I spoke to them, and they rushed right over, and we're introducing themselves to Detective Iturbi when I came into the living room. Bob asked Iturbi, could he see the letter before he took it for evidence. When he saw it, he said something that I thought was strange.

He said, "I knew it would just be a matter of time before someone tried to do something to you. I don't understand how you could sing so well after so long without practicing everyday. We've worked with the best singers in the world.

You guys have seen all the preparation it takes for these singers to keep up with their voices. Anybody would think that you made a deal with the Devil, or something.

I mean, I've had weird thoughts about you, and I'm one of your best friends.

We all just looked at him for a while without saying a word. Then I asked Bob, "where did I get the devil's number to ask for the deal, the yellow pages."

Everyone just laughed, except Iturbi. He asked Bob, "where were you last night, and do you have an alibi?"

Bob said "I was guarding Paris Hilton last night, is that good enough for you?"

Iturbi said, "I'll check it out too".

Then Iturbi started to speak, and his demeanor got very serious, "look you guys, this guy is serious".

"He picked the lock in here like a professional, and came into a house with a known Martial Arts expert, and didn't care"."

This person can handle himself, and has been around violence."

"He is serious about his threats." "He probably knows how to use weapons too".

"Don't underestimate this person. Alright?" "I'm out of here. I'll be in touch".

Bob, and Albert both said in unison, "I like that guy."

Two months went by, and I was to start a United States concert tour. In that time nothing happened out of the ordinary. There wasn't any contact whatsoever from this nut case. I decided to take my whole family on tour with me so they could be kept safe. I thought maybe we could get close again, like we used to be.I hired Albert, and Bob, full time and they went everywhere with my wife, and children.

The first stop on the tour was New York City. I had an apartment set up for me, and the family to stay in whenever we come to NYC. It was in Queens. I was trying to stay closer to my parents, and brother. I bought a house for them in Queens.

One of Sony's biggest studio's was in New York, and I knew I had to spend a lot of time there, so I purchased an apartment in Midtown Manhattan also. It had all the comforts of home, and was right near all the movies, and a half mile from Broadway. Only a few choice family members, and friends knew about this place. My record company, and voice teacher knew also.

When we got to the airport, we were mobbed by fans. They knew the exact time of arrival. I signed some autographs while the family made it to the limos. Once they were safely in the car, I made my move to the car too. I sat down next to my wife, and as I tried to get comfortable,

My Son says, "Hey dad, what's that big letter sticking out of your pocket?"

I reached in my pocket, and there sure was a letter there, and with my name on it.

It was a plain white envelope with a little bulge in it that was very small, so I did't feel like it was anything that could hurt us.

I thought it was most likely a letter from a group-y or something with her phone number on it.

That kind of stuff has happened before.

So I say out loud, "it must be some young girl trying to hit on pops" ya know I still got it" !

Katherine grabs the letter out my hand and say's "I'll take care of this for you"

Let's see what kind of fan mail you've been getting. There is a little lump in it. My daughter says, "it must be some girl's panties.

When my wife opens the letter, there was a piece of an ear, pressed as flat as it could get. No blood, just a piece of someone's ear.

Katherine let out a little shrill scream, as she realized what she had pulled out from the letter.

The driver pulled over when he heard the scream, and asked if everything was alright. I said, "Call the police, and have them meet us at the apartment".

I read the note, and what it said. It almost put me into shock.

It said, "here is a little keepsake from your good friend, and Co-star Jasmine Love. Now you both will never be apart".

I wanted to scream also, but nothing would come out. I couldn't believe this beautiful young woman, with her whole life ahead of her, was taken away because of me. I knew she had to be dead. I felt a sickness in my stomach so bad, that I had to get out of the car on the highway and throw-up. I already knew from this point, that this person, if I got my way, wasn't going to trial.

Everyone thought Jasmine was in Paris on vacation. I had been keeping up with her whereabouts since that night. No one had said she was missing. I pulled up Detective Iturbi's phone number in L. A., and told him what just happened, and asked him to check Jasmine's home.

By the time we arrived at our New York apartment, Iturbi had already discovered her body. Her airplane ticket was on her dining room table. Her packed bags were waiting at the door. The New York Police were at my apartment too. I gave them the contents of the envelope, and told them the whole story from the beginning, and that this started in California. I gave them Iturbi's number but they said that since this person is following me across the country, that they had to call the FBI.

I still was in disbelief. This person knew about me and Jasmine. He saw us make love. When my wife, and the police asked about the note, and what this person meant by, "now we would never be apart."

"I told them that this idiot must think the love scene that me and Jasmine played in the movie was real, and that this person has got to be crazy to believe a movie". They went for it.

Only me, Jasmine, and the killer knew what really happened. How, I do not know. We were in the room alone for days. I know this nut couldn't have been watching me and Jasmine in the hotel room. We hadn't planned what happened but it wasn't hard to guess what we were doing if he had followed us there. This person saw everyone come out of the room but me, and her, and then waited for days outside, this asshole was really sick and had it out for me. Also, this person got close enough to stick a letter in my pocket without me feeling it in that crowd.

Maybe someone saw the person put it in my pocket. With all those camera's flashing, someone might have gotten a picture. If the police didn't get this guy, and I had a chance, I wanted to kill this son of a bitch.

16
CHAPTER

Sony, and I, decided to put the tour off for a month, so things could be worked out for the protection of me, and my family. We all had flown back to California the next day to try to get a fix on things. Plus, I had to attend Jasmine's funeral which was coming up in a couple of days. I left my family in the hands of some other bodyguards I knew, while Bob, Albert, and I decided to go work out a little, and get some frustration off of us.

I didn't give any slack to them this time. I took all my frustrations out on them, not to where I hurt them or anything, I just let them know who was the best. They were kind of upset and said they were going to the store to get some juice and that they would be right back.

When they left, I started thinking about Jasmine. How I would never feel her in my arms again. Even though it was a one time thing, I knew that if I changed my mind, she would be there. Now she was gone forever, because of me, because I didn't have the guts years ago to stay with what I loved. My music. Now my voice got some people killed. I started feeling unsure of myself like I did in my younger days.

I walked to the other side of the gym, and started doing some breathing exercises. Then some Police officers, and some FBI agents showed up that were somewhat involved in my case. They knew I was at the gym, and they figured since they heard about my Martial Arts skills, they would try me out since they were assigned to be around me from time to time anyway. The officers that knew me, figured that I must be rusty, while the ones that didn't know me, thought that all this Martial Arts stuff was hype for my acting career.

I went to their asses, one at a time with ease. They were all very impressed with my skills. I took a break, and started to do breathing exercises, when the finest women I had ever saw walked into the gym. I mean she was finer than Jasmine, Katherine and most women I had seen in my life to that point. I couldn't believe my eyes. I looked over at the other officers in the gym to see if they were seeing what I was seeing. I noticed they were laughing, and were pulling out money like they were betting on something.

I thought to myself that this was some kind of joke bringing this fine woman in here.

She was also walking straight for me.

She was tall, and got taller as she got closer. When she reached me, she was about an inch taller than me. She was long, and lanky, like a model except she was thick. She was built tight, with thick long legs, and a huge chest for her size. I mean her chest was perfect, it wasn't really that it was big. It's that it was healthy, and pointing straight at me, which made it look like it was huge.

They were 38c's.

She was about 38, 22, 32. Her skin was smooth, and her bronze complexion seemed to glow about her. Her facial features were exact, and precisely chiseled in line. Nose perfect, lips robust, but not so much so. Her eyes were light brown and could drown you in thought. Her legs were long, and strong looking, like she could squeeze you to death if she wanted to. She had a tattoo on her right ankle of a red rose, with a dagger through it. On the other leg was a little scar right above the knee that was somehow very exciting.

She comes right up to my face, nose to nose and says, "you what to spar?"

I knew this was a joke for sure. I said to her, "who put your fine ass up to this?"

She looked at me real cold and said, "no one, do you want to spar wimp singer, actor. You can't act your way through this ass whooping."

I looked over at the guys and said, "What's this about guys?"

"I'm not in the mood"." "I don't care how fine she is",

"I'll throw her around the room",

"so you better come get her".

When I said that,She grabbed me in a judo hold, and threw me across the mat. Everyone started laughing.

I said to myself, "what the fuck!"

I'm gonna kick her fine ass too like I did everybody else in here, I just don't care who I beat on today. I grabbed her by her arm, and she pulled me towards her using my force against me, and threw me to the mat again. As the guys started laughing again, I realize they brought in this fox, that can really fight, and were betting that she would kick my ass. I raise myself up off the mat real slow and start talking to this women.

"So you got some skills huh",

"well I'm gonna have to teach you a lesson foxy".

She then grabs me again, throws me to the mat and says, "Are you gonna fight, or talk me to death?"

When I got up, I threw her around, and she returned the favor. She was really good. I was better, but not by much. In the end, I prevailed, and made a new friend in the process. When I asked her her name, she said a name that fit her beauty, and talent so well, it was like meeting a cartoon character or something. Her name was Anise. The name of a beautiful, mysterious, warrior women. After we traded numbers, she said she would see me soon, and just left the gym the same way she came.

17
CHAPTER

When Albert and Bob showed up, I said, ? "What took you guys so long?"

"I can't believe you missed everything that just happened in here".

I couldn't stop talking about Anise. It was just like I was a kid in School again. I could't get her out of my mind. I told them all I knew, and bragged about how she beat me up. The way I described her, they wouldn't have believed me if the other officers didn't back up my story. Everyone said the same thing about her. They said she just appears out of the blue once a week, and never really lets anyone know anything about her.

Then she leaves just as mysteriously as she shows up, but does not leave until she beats everyone up in the gym.

The guys say I'm the only one that ever beat her. Other guys say that she was holding back, and gave me a real ass whooping. I told them that I was holding back too. Albert and Bob really wanted me too. They had never seen anyone beat on me like they heard Anise did.

Bob said "maybe we will see her another time, remember we are leaving after the show in two days."

I said "well maybe next time.

Back at the hotel, my wife, and children had heard about the women that kicked my ass, and were joking from the minute I got in. They got quite a laugh out of it because of the way I always brag to them that no one can kick my ass. We were having a great time laughing and joking until the phone rang.

Sergeant Iturbi was on the line. "Hello Gerald! How are you, and the family doing?"

"I didn't mean to disturb you all but there is some information I must share with you right away".

"Your daughter's boyfriend was found murdered."

"It was the same way your Co-star was murdered."

"With piano wire, and burnt with lighter fluid."

"I was checking on the computer to see if any other similar crimes had been committed anywhere, and I got a hit".

"Apparently, an old lady in a nursing home was tied with piano wire, and burnt alive."

"When I checked further, I found she taught at the same Junior High you went to, and that she was also your music teacher when you were a child."

"This is no coincidence." I said, "that must have been Ms. Grossman they found."

"According to the nurses, they claim someone that looked just like you had visited her some time before she was killed".

"You flew to New York on business back then, I checked."

"You were the only visit she had in years, that's why they remembered you."

"You won American Idol a year later."

"The people that knew you when you were a child said, you were meant to be famous."

"What happened back then, that made you stop singing, and acting, when so many people are telling me that you were the best they ever heard or saw act from a child?"

"What stopped you back then"? "And what made you unleash this talent so late in life, and right after you visited your old teacher?"

I told him the whole story. He couldn't believe I could let someone stop me from my destiny.

I told him, "Look Iturbi, things have happened the way it's supposed to be."

"What is meant to be, is meant to be".

"It's God's plan for the universe, and we can't change anything." I thought about it for a long time. These children I have, my friends, the life I've led, are all for a reason."

"I still don't understand why things happened in this order, but it did."

"I wouldn't have had this special time, with this beautiful wife of mine, and known what love is like in this way".

"Shoot, I might not have loved at all, or lived for that matter."

"Things would be different."

Iturbi said, "Well, things are much more serious than we thought. Security has to be beefed up, and a plan has to be made to lure this guy in".

'He, or she, has it out for you, but they seem like they want to get to you through your acquaintances."

"I can't cover everyone you know."

"Only you, and your immediate family, and that's not gonna be easy."

"So Gerald, I am going to get with your people, and see what we can come up with."

"I want to know when anyone goes to the store or goes anywhere."

"Anytime anyone leaves the house, someone will have to be with you all."

"Phone calls have to be monitored and people that are coming and going in and out of here must be screened and checked out Got that?"

I said yea, "I got it!"

I waited until the next day to tell my wife, and children, what Iturbi and I had talked about. No sense in not letting them get a good night's sleep, and I was right to do so. When they heard what had happened, everyone was in a panic. My daughter was all to pieces. Everyone was really scared now, and I was really frightened for the safety of my family. The FBI was assigned to my case now.

After my talk with Iturbi, he figured the regular police was not enough so he called the FBI. I was waiting to meet the new agent in charge that the FBI was sending over.

They say this agents name was Chandler, and that he was the best they had for these kinds of situations. I felt good about that. It made me feel like my government really cared about my families welfare and safety.

Bob and Albert were out of town until the next day, but when they returned, I would have them, and FBI agents for my family, and myself. This should make things real hard for this nut.

One hour later, the FBI shows up. To my surprise, it was Anise. She was the FBI agent in charge. Before I could say anything to her, she asked if she could talk to me alone. We went into the kitchen and she started talking.

"Look Gerald, I don't want anyone to know that you know me, or that it was me that you fought in the gym."

"At this point everyone is a suspect to me",

"and one of my advantages with this killer is that he doesn't know that I can break his back with my bare hands."

"So let's not tell anybody, anything, including your bodyguard friends" Understand?" I told her,

"I couldn't feel any safer than what I feel right now that you came in".

"I know what you can do".

"They say you're the best, and at least with your hands and feet I know they are right."

"We'll keep everything secret".

So now, there were a bunch of us that I knew could beat this guy half to death. If I couldn't get my hands on this guy, I know she would. Then there was Bob and Albert.

Between all of us, we were in great shape.

I called her Agent Chandler, and Katherine, and my children took to her right away. She made us feel safe with her knowledge, and personality. I felt really blessed to have her, and I knew that Our encounter at the gym was an act of fate somehow. I made up my mind to start paying more attention to the spiritual side of life from this point. I wanted to read more about how The Lord worked, because this meeting with Anise was not an accident.

Bob, and Albert, when they saw Agent Chandler,were smitten by her beauty right away, but they immediately dismissed her ability to protect me and the family. They felt that if she didn't get the drop on the killer with her weapon, that she was dead. They just didn't know what she was capable of. She had them all fooled with her charm and beauty. They thought she was soft and that she was one of those women that slept her way into this job. This was exactly what she wanted everyone around me to think, and it worked better than we could have ever imagined.

18

CHAPTER

The tour was to start at the Virginia Beach Amp-ha Theater. It was a outdoor theater, and it wasn't going to be easy to guard anyone there. Still, the show must go on as they say. The whole family was going to attend this concert, and my children didn't want to sit with their mother because, they said they couldn't party like they wanted to around mom, so Bob said He would hang with them the entire show. Security, and the FBI agreed it shouldn't be to hard keeping on eye on everyone because, the show wouldn't go on as long in Virginia, being Everything closed down early in VA. They had most things closed by 2 am. Sunday, through Thursday, even earlier.

My voice always felt stronger after 8 PM, so I didn't want to start a show before that time, so that I could give a good performance for my fans. Unfortunately, because they closed everything earlier in Virginia, Virginia had had other Ideas about a start time. They insisted the show start at 6 PM so they could shut the concert down no later than 12 am. So we complied if there was to be a show.

Virginia also had a big Religious base, so I wanted to comply to whatever requirements they asked of me. They didn't have a lot of big named entertainers come down there like other places such as New York, Chicago, or Los Angeles, because to the strick way they carried their city, plus they didn't have the big arenas like the other cities, so an entertainer had to do more shows to reach his fan base. People couldn't enjoy themselves as much either because of strict laws. They couldn't smoke marijuana, or drink as freely as the bigger cities, which for me in my situation made me feel more comfortable as far as watching out for my wife, and children. When people are real drunk they, sometimes try to run up on the stage and grab you. They mean well, but they sometimes hurt the entertainer.

Virginia was the kind of place you wanted to live at if you did't have any bad habits, and were a straight living kind of person. If you had bad habits, VA was not for you. Your going to jail.

Albert was going to watch over Katherine, while the FBI was concentrating on me mostly. I had Anise hanging around me, and checking on the wife, and children also. She was overly concerned, and really wanted my people to cancel the show, but it just wasn't feasible.

The place was sold out months ahead of time, as well as all the other shows in other cities, and The schedule had to be followed to the letter. I felt that I was the main target now, and that my wife, and children, were no longer the main focus of the killer.

Anise felt different about the killer's intentions. She felt the person wanted to go after my family to hurt me, and was saving me for last.

As the show got closer, and the crowd got bigger, she decided to put more security around my wife, and children.

The show went well, and it was a real pleasure to do. My family had a great time, and enjoyed all the songs, and dancing that went on in the show. After the show, Anise pulled a surprise on us, and had us whisked off to the airport. All our clothes were packed while the show was on, and taken to the airport. The plane was already fueled, and ready for departure.

The summer went on, and the tour was a great success. With my family being with me, we were a cohesive unit once more. We hadn't heard anything from the killer for the rest of the tour. No notes, no contact of any kind. I was kind of praying he was just dead somewhere. Hit by a truck, or something, but I kept telling myself that in the movies, the bad guy never just has an accident and dies. It never works out that way, so I still needed to beware. He had killed people, and deep inside I wanted to kill him myself. I knew it was wrong to think like that. The Bible says, God fights your battles, but if this person was within my hands grasp, I don't know what I would do. I knew I would be eternally grateful if he was dead somewhere.

The last show was at the L.A. Forum in Anaheim, California. The place was going to be full of celebrates from all over Hollywood, and the world. My dressing room was full if flowers, and candy, and other assorted goodies. The FBI was examining everything that came in.

There were also letters, and invitations to parties, and all types of things. My dressing room was packed to the hilt. My voice felt exceptionally strong, and I was going to make this last show the best of all for the finale to a great tour.

I was looking forward to taking a break from all entertainment for a couple of weeks, so I had to make this show powerful, so people would want more and be anxious for my return. Hopefully they would be dying for my break to end so they could get more of my music So I knew I couldn't take to long a break especially being a relatively new artist.

Katherine wanted to go to a Island Hotel, with no television, or radio, and just talk, and make love. Just me and her. Bathe in clear blue water, and heal. Just the sound of the sea waves coming up on the shore would do wonders for me and the Mrs. As soon as this show was over, and I cleared up a couple of things, I was gonna surprise Katherine and take her away to Tahiti.

Just me and her, where no one would be close enough to mess with us. No children, no Sony people or crazy people. If this killer followed us all the way to Tahiti, almost the other side of the world from here, it would be easy for him to get caught. Even he or she would have to wait until I got back to mess with me. I'll have twenty-four hour a day bodyguards around my children so everything should be alright. Katherine and I need to get away a take a good hard look at all the changes that have happen and come up with some kind of plan to deal with our knew life so we can all cope with each other and the changes that have occurred.

I was looking forward to this trip.

When the show began, the lights were out all over the arena, which didn't sit well with Anise, especially since this wasn't the procedure in any other show. This show was different because my promoters wanted to go out with a bang, so when the lights did finally come on, I was to be lowered onto the stage in a chariot.

I admit it was awesome, but dangerous.

As the crowd waited for the lights to come on, I started singing. The crowd went wild. Then only a spot light came on, lighting up the chariot in the air. As the noise level lifted, people started running up to the stage in droves. Security, and Albert, tried to contend with the rush of people rushing out of their seats. They lost sight of Katherine for just a minute, and that was all it took.

When they finally caught sight of her, she was reaching towards her back, and yelling for help. The noise drowned the sounds of her plea for help. Albert saw her, and thought she was trying to scratch her back at first, until she dropped to her knees. As Albert ran towards her, she was reaching for something behind her in desperation. As Albert got closer he saw there was a knife sticking out of Katherine's back.

Immediately he got on the radio, and reported Katherine down. He called for an ambulance. He knew it would take to long for the ambulance to reach her through the crowd, so he lifted her up over his shoulder, and jogged to the nearest exit. The crowd didn't notice a thing, and no one told me anything. They rushed Katherine to the hospital and didn't tell me anything until after the show was over. They claimed they didn't want to start a riot, or stampede of people. The children were brought to the hospital with their mother so they could be secured, and also to be with their mother in case she wanted her family around.

When I arrived, the children thought I was told about Katherine, and chose to keep singing in the show.

They just looked at me, and ran out of the hospital. I asked Bob and Albert, "where is Katherine?"

They both looked at me with this look that I'll never forget. I knew what they were going to say before they said it. As I dropped to my knees in pain, I heard the words. Katherine, my lovely wife was gone. I didn't know what to do, or think. After a moment, I asked where she was. She is still in the hospital ER Bob said. When I got there, I asked to be alone. with her before they took her.

I held her lifeless body, and cried. All warmth gone. The soul that brought life to her body had passed on. All that was left, was a shell of the beauty that bore me my children, and gave me so much happiness. I had seen and felt death before with relatives, but never had anyone passed this close to me. There was no one as close to me in the world as she was. Not even my parents or children. She was my heart. I was dead inside, and lost.

The news was all over the air waves, and the news media were unforgiving in their pursuit for an interview with me. They stationed themselves all around the house, especially in my driveway so I couldn't move my car without them seeing me. The phone rang off the hook, so I just pulled the phone out of the wall, turned off all the lights, and sat in my big chair in the living room until I pass out. I was alone. Instead of my children coming to the house so we could all be together in this terrible time, they stayed away. Blaming my fame for their mother's death. They were right too. If I wasn't singing, none of this would have happened. I thought to myself how my voice has somehow been more of a curse to me than a gift.

Once again I didn't want to sing, but I couldn't let this guy win. Also, Mr. Jakes, and everyone else in the whole world were saying how much of a gift my voice was to them.

I sure was confused at this stage of my life as to God's plan for me. So I just prayed and asked for help and guidance.

I stayed in silence for days, not eating or drinking anything. Midnight of the third day, someone was breaking in the back door of my house. I went to the door weak, but hoping it was that asshole, so I could kill him. I reached in my hallway desk for the 9mm I kept there.

Then the lock turned. I waited to see who was dumb enough to come into my house now. Then I heard a voice before the door opened. It was Anise. She said, "I know you are standing at the door with your weapon. "It's Anise! I'm worried about you, I brought you some food."

I told her, "come in since you already broke in." I wouldn't have accepted anyone else in the world to do something like this at this time in my life. I knew if I tried to fight her as weak as I was, she would fire me up. So I just accepted her offerings.

She filled me in on what they thought happened. There were no witnesses of course with all the commotion of the show. She assured me that no press would get to me until I was ready. She told me, "Gerald, Your famous, and with fame comes people being in your Kool-Aid all the time".

"At some point you're going to have to make a statement."

"After you do that, the crowd will die down a tad, but the questions about this situation won't die for along time, so get prepared for that."

"Your life is not your own."

"People think they know you". "They love you."

"Some even want to help you find Katherine's murderer", and we will use any information we can to find this bastard". "He might not make it to a trial."

I looked at her and said, "did you understand what you just said to me"?

"Cause if I get this person alone, they ain't going to no trial, I promise you."

To my surprise she said, "those are my intentions if we can get away with it".

"I liked Katherine and your whole family."

"I know this is not the time, but I think you kind of know how I feel about you."

I just looked at her speechless. It was the wrong time, but I felt confused because, I loved my wife, and yet there was something for Anise.

I looked at her and said, "It is the wrong time, but I'm glad you got it out now so we can concentrate on the task at hand."

"Only time will tell what happens between us, but I'm not on that page right now".

"Understand"? She replied, "of-course! "Won't mention it again!"

I had made up my mind to kill this bastard if I could get away with it, no matter what. I asked Anise to always keep me updated at all times. Anytime she got some news on the killer of my wife, I wanted to know about it right away.

She told me, "I'll keep you involved as long as you keep your head on straight".

She said, "If you ever lose it Gerald, you're out".

I didn't want her to know my intentions about killing this sucker, she might think I was using her to get to the killer. I wasn't. I was using everybody I knew in law enforcement to keep me abreast so I could get him or her.

I told her, "I respect what you're doing for me, and I would never be a hindrance to you, or the investigation."

Anise then said, "I'll keep you around since you're the only one that is close to my skill level in Martial Arts."

"I'll be able to stay sharp using you as a test dummy."

"I replied, "I Was holding back that day".

"I could beat you anytime I wanted to." She said, "Whatever!"

Months had gone by, and the killer didn't show his ugly face. No notes, no letters, no nothing.

Not a word. There weren't any clues, and things were looking dismal as far as catching this son of a bitch. I was spending a lot of time with Anise, and that was the only positive thing that seemed to be happening at the time. Anise was allot more woman than she appeared to be from the outside. She was a great cook, and a very good painter. She practiced her Martial Arts every morning, and that kept me sharp too. She also had a B. A. from Howard University for Criminal Psychology, and had a very good personality. She could be very funny when she wanted to be.

She told me this silly joke about two whales. A Husband, and Wife, whale couple. Well the husbands whale father, was killed by whaler seaman, and the husband wanted revenge on the seaman that killed his father. One day while the husband whale was swimming with his wife and they spotted the ship of the seaman that killed his father. The husband asked his wife to help him destroy the ship.

They were to swim under the ship, and use their blowholes to flip the ship, and drown the seaman. So the wife agreed, and they did just that. They drown the seaman, but as they were swimming away, they noticed that some survived. The husband asked the wife to turn around and eat them up. The wife looks at her husband and say's, "'That's enough!

"I helped you blow them", "but I'm not going to swallow the seaman".

It was such a corny joke it made me laugh non stop for a while. She had a lot of dry jokes like that. She would talk to me all the time about the beauty of life and I grew fonder and fonder of her with each passing day.

Then the day came when she told me how she felt again except this time she was passionate about it.

"Gerald, I know we said we would talk about feelings later, but I have to tell you before I bust inside."

"I need you in my life, and I'm willing to wait as long as it takes for you."

I said, "Anise I feel the same way, it's just going to take some time to feel right about this feeling I have for you". "I know Katherine is gone, just give me time."

"As long as it takes Gerald!" "I'm waiting to take your pain away."

Wow! I couldn't believe what was happening. To make things even more beautiful, it was such a beautiful day weather wise. It was about seventy-five degrees. There was a light breeze blowing which made her long dark hair move like an animated flower in a movie. It magnified the situation, and had me praying for a solution. I contacted T.D. Jakes and asked if I could come see him. I needed help in reaching closure between me and Katherine.

I met with him the next week for lunch, and told him my problem. Had enough time went by to stop grieving for my wife? This was the question that was eating at my heart because I couldn't get past the guilt I felt for her death.

I didn't even go to my hotel to check in. I went right to T.D. Jakes who was meeting me in a restaurant in downtown Dallas. He was dressed casual, in a sweat suit, and sneakers, as was I. I told him my dilemma and he looked me in the eyes for a minute, then started to talk.

"Look Gerald!" "You were blessed with great talent".

"You were blessed with a great wife that brought you through the time of you finding yourself so you could use the talent God gave you."

"You probably weren't ready to deal with fame at a young age"

"and God let you bring it out now".

"The life you had with Katherine was meant to be lived the way it was."

"She was put in your life because that's what you needed to reach the place you are at now."

"Your children were born from your love with her, and your daughter that was made through your love with Katherine was responsible for your getting on American Idol."

"All things already written in God's Plan Book".

"Now unfortunately things have happened the way they have."

"You weren't left here to go out like a punk." "You're supposed to stay strong for you, and the memory of Katherine, your children, and the world, as an inspiration of how to stay strong in adversity".

"You can't let some crazed fool dictate the course of your life and world."

"Then every time someone doesn't like something about someone, All they have to do is start hurting the people around them to get what they want."

"Every nut might start doing that then". "That's why people fight back".

"That's why there is good and evil."

Evil never wins against good." "God dictates the course of all of our lives, not some nut".

"Believe in God and keep the Faith". "You will prevail, and like Job, you will end up with even more than what you had before".

"Trust in him. God has blessed you with a soul mate that will get you through these hard times, and she can protect herself as well as you."

"There is a reason for that too".

"Maybe she's going to get this killer."

"Just continue to live and stay faithful and strong and get into God Word".

"There is a story for every situation in the Good Book. "God has plans for you."

"Pray before you make any moves and The Lord will guide you through all your life, Good and Bad."

That night as I slept, MyKatherine gave me the answer. I dreamt about her in college where we met. She was wearing a beautiful white dress with green polka dots and she was dancing around me. "Gerald I'm alright, your destiny was not with me as you will see."

"We had a special love, but the Lord has something else for you to do."

"Follow your heart always, and do what you were meant to do, sing".

"Your a good man, and you were my reward for my time on earth, and I Thank God for every moment with you."

"Enjoy your life, and live it to the fullest"

"Anise lovesyou, and you love her too." "Go for it!"

I woke up and called Anise to tell her my dream but she wasn't home. As I came out of the bathroom from brushing my teeth, there was a knock at the door. It was Anise. As I opened the door she just walked past me and let herself in. She started talking right away before I could say a word about the dream I had.

She said, "You know how I feel about you, but there is more."

"I loved you from the first time we fought in the gym."

"I respected your marriage always, and would never try to interfere, but now we are here in love".

"I never wanted anything to happen to Katherine, I liked her as a friend, and she was good for you".

"I know that she would tell you herself that I could be good for you if you would give me a chance."

"There is no one for me in this world but you."

"We have so many things in common, and I want you."

"God has dealt a different hand for both of us that we didn't expect, or hope for."

"Now a year has gone by, and I have to express my feelings for you, and with all due respect, It's time to move on."

"I know Katherine will always be in your memories."

"Please don't ever try to extinguish her memory".

"I would never expect that from you, and wouldn't ever dream of forgetting her myself".

"She was beautiful in heart, mind, spirit, and beauty." "She was the mother of your children."

"As long as she was alive, I would have never told anyone about my feelings for you, and would have given up any chance of being with you".

"I would have moved on."

"But, things have happened the way they have." "No fault of ours."

"This nutcase did this. Not me."

"Not your fame. A nut!"

"You have mourned her like a good husband, and know it's time for you to move on."

"Katherine would want that". "I know that much about her." "Tell me I'm wrong"

I said, "You're right, she would want me to be happy."

I do have feelings for you, but is it fair to you?"

"Are we hooking up because of the situation of going through these murders together and spending so much time together?" "We are both alone.

She said, "I thought everything through already". "We are so much alike, and you know, and feel the same thing, and the same way I do".

"This is just how things are." "God has put us together to get through all this".

"He doesn't make mistakes." "We are meant to be together".

"I'll make you happy. You have someone right in front of you that's willing to help you through these hard times, and create our own good times in the process".

"I love you!"

"Will you give me a chance to make you happy"

When she said that, she grabbed me, pulled me towards her, and kissed me with those beautiful full lips. We started helping each other with the removal of our clothes. We made passionate love, that was so good it surpassed Yasmine Love. I not only found love again so soon, but with a bonus. The bonus was the sex being more than I could have bargained for. I had someone more exciting than Yasmine, and some-one that I felt some kind of spiritual connection to. This was the feeling of completion in a relationship. I felt a fullness that I never felt with Katherine. I wouldn't think it possible to love again and stronger than before, let alone love someone and feel so complemented and complete. My appreciation for love was more than before. I kind of took it for granted. Not again. God was surely good.

20
CHAPTER

We tried to keep our relationship quiet for the children's sake, until I could talk to them, and get them to stop blaming me for not being with Katherine when she died. She had never regained consciousness, so she didn't get to say goodbye, or see anybody before she died, and yet they still felt anger towards me.

Looking back on the situation, my handlers were right. People might have gotten hurt, and more people would have died besides Katherine if I would left the stage in the middle of the show. Most people wouldn't care, and I wouldn't have been able to handle more people being hurt on account of me. I didn't tell Anise my dream of Katherine at that time because I had realized that the way things turned out was of Gods design, and I didn't feel insecure anymore about my talent, or the way things had turned out. This was just the way things were meant to be.

Despite how much we tried, the news people caught wind of our relationship, and started gossiping in the papers. We were all over the papers, and in magazines, and jokes on late night T.V. They were saying how the FBI always gets their man. I mean they were terrible.

Anise's boss wanted her to resign with full benefits of-course, and I agreed. Two months later I asked her to marry me. That's when the letters came.

Anise and I had gone to the park for a walk, and then we went shopping. When we returned to our house, there was a letter under the door. It was written the same way as the other's. It said, "congratulations on your new relationship. I see you found a new member spawned from Satan himself."

"I'll make sure that this one dies in more pain than the last. Then I'll come after you, voice from hell."

The FBI found no clues whatsoever. This person left no fingerprints, hair fibers, nothing. Iturbi was still hanging around, and had become a friend. I saw him, and Bob, and Albert, about the same amount of time. They were right in the mix of things, but I was starting to feel like this killer was close to me and Albert let Katherine get stabbed, or did he. Maybe he stabbed her? The questions have been asked over, and over, in my mind.

I didn't want to believe it, but the thought had been eating away at me for a long time. I told Iturbi how I felt, and we had Albert watched around the clock.

I sure didn't know my buddy had such a giving life outside his job. He didn't do anything but go to church, and workout. He didn't have any women, or love life at all. He was boring as far as what you would think the life would be like for a bodyguard of big stars would be. There was no action or drama at all. He did the same thing over and over like he was an old man set in his ways.

Something was filling his life because he always seemed happy.

The agents followed him to a place with orphaned children. He was teaching the children Bible Stories. The agents said they sat in the audience with the other adults and listened.

He told the story of David and Goliath. He told them that story so they wouldn't be afraid of bigger people, or the odds being against them in life. He Albert said to them, "You must know the Lord God is on your side when you are in the right."

"You must keep the faith so that you win the righteous battle against evil."

"Never be afraid of scary looking, big people".

He said, "there once was a boy named David." "He was a sheep herder, and singer of songs".

"He believed in God, and Loved God more than his own life."

"He thanked God every single day for the good, and the bad, that happened in his life."

"Why"? "Because he knew that the bad things were lessons to make him stronger."

"He knew that God was all knowing, and trusted in His judgment, even though he couldn't see God".

"He felt God's presence in the Air, the earth, and sea, and in all things around him."

"He knew God was with him always."

"There was a big war going on at the time with the Philistines, and the Israelites".

"David was an Israelite, and had some brothers fighting for them."

"He was too young to fight so his father had him home tending the sheep."

"So David's way of helping was to bring food for his brothers to the battlefield when the "fighting stopped." "This day, David's father sent some food with David to the battle field, and David heard this big ugly giant down in the valley daring anyone to come fight him." "He was "nine feet tall and had a spear that was longer than anyone had ever seen before." "His sword was almost as big as some of the Israelites".

"All the Israelites were scared of the big giant". What they forgot was that fear is a trick of the devil".

"One that really believes in God has no one to fear because, The Lord will help you fight your battles."

"Sometimes he doesn't help in the way you would like, but he is always there when you believe in him".

"Because these Israelites didn't believe like they should. They didn't have the faith that David had."

"When David heard the giant Goliath daring any Israelite to fight them, and no one answered the call."

"David got mad and yelled out the Israelites on the battlefield, "who is this heathen that would talk likethis to God's people in this manner?"

'Why is it that no one has answered this challenge? Goliath said again, "Are there no champions in this battlefield that will face me?" "David couldn't take this giants mouth anymore." "He couldn't take the fact that no one stood up to this giant to represent the God that he loved, and believed in so much."

So David said to King Saul, "I will go and fight this heathen."

Saul said, "you are just a boy! "How can you fight a professional soldier that is proven in the battlefield?"

David said, "when bears, and lions, attacked my sheep, I faced them, and slew them with the help of God".

"He will not let me down this time either."

The King said, "Give this lad some armor, and a sword, and let him fight on behalf of our people."

"When David came out on the battlefield, his armor was hanging off his butt like the way you all wear your jeans, and he could hardly lift the sword they gave him."

The children got a laugh out of that, imagining how David looked with his armor hanging down past his butt, so Albert had to wait until they stopped laughing before he could continue. When they stopped laughing,he continued the story.

Well, David said to himself, "I can't wear this armor, it's gonna get me killed."

"I'll fight the way the Lord had me fight Lions and Bears." "With my sling-shot!"

So David looked around the battlefield for some sharp, good slinging rocks, and started talking to Goliath.

"Goliath, who do you think you are coming down here to my neighborhood trying to run Something?

"This is my Lord's block! "You better leave now before I go upside your head".

Goliath started laughing and said, "you ain't nothing but a little boy".

He looked up at all the Israelis and said, "you disrespect me by sending a boy to fight me."

"This is all you have. Punks!" David said, "what it is punk, is that we felt since we believe in God so much, we didn't need to send no one but a boy to handle you sucker."

David then said, "Stop talking me to death, we gonna fight or are you gonna talk me to death.?"

Then Goliath threw the spear he had at David and missed. When the spear went by David's head, it made a big whistling sound because it was so big. David said, "That's all you got, big guy?"

Then David took one of his rocks out of his pouch, and hit Goliath right between the eyes and knocked the the giant out. Then he took Goliath's sword, and cut his head off. All the Philistines ran away. A little boy defeated a giant because The Lord gave him the means to win by showing him to have faith, and have no fear.

That story was so beautifully told that it was hard to think of him as a suspect anymore. Along with the fact that he didn't do anything but help kids and go home, then back to work everyday.

Later that week, Albert came to my house and said that he needed to talk to me alone. I brought him into my study, and he looked me in my eyes and said, "look Gerald, I didn't kill Katherine."

"I would never hurt anyone in your family."

"I've noticed those guys following me, and I understand how I could be a suspect, especially with everyone knowing how I feel about you being able to sing so well after all these years of not practicing, but I'm not a crazed maniac."

"So they need to spend their time, and money, finding the real killer, and stop wasting taxpayers money."

"Yes, I've been open about how I feel amongst us here, and that's as far as it goes."

"I love you like a brother."

"You are family, and your family is my family also". "So please stop."

"I believe it's someone close to us all too".

"It's someone that acts like they are your friend, and love's your voice, but really hates you."

"I don't hate anyone, let alone you."

"Whoever it is, they know our schedule." "When we go to the store, every move."

"We need to sit down and really think."

"I want to bring closure to this person's existence."

I started to feel sorry for the killer if any of us caught this person.

It didn't seem like anyone around me wanted this bastard to make it to trial.

I told Albert that I believed him, but that in the police's mind, everyone is a suspect. I asked them to to stop following him, and they believed that he wasn't the one, but they were not going to Take him off the suspect list.

Once again, time went by with no new notes, or any clues whatsoever.

Things seemed calm for the moment, that's when you really had to be on guard. There was always calm before a storm. So Anise and I stayed sharp.

21
CHAPTER

My son Louis, and daughter Maria, were still not talking to me, and were doing drugs at a fierce pace. They were staying in San Francisco, and were going off. They both were together in San Francisco, and we're messing up tough. I had detective's following them around the clock to make sure they were safe. They were taking LSD, sniffing cocaine, and doing every drug that was put in front of them. They were not famous, so they were not really known, so the people they were hanging with didn't recognize them.

I had the detective's just observe. No contact unless they were in harm's way.

I told only a few people that I hired detective's to let everyone close feel better, as well as myself. Months had gone by once again, no notes, no incidents.

I was doing a little acting now, and things seemed to be lightened a bit. That's when the kids decided to come home. They looked terrible. They told me that they were sorry for the way they had acted, and they told me about the drugs and wanted help. They said some man kept giving them whatever they wanted drug wise, and that's why they never called for money. Louis said"pops! you should have seen this dude man."

"He was shaped so funny." "He was old and bald, and it seemed that when we ran out of drugs, he would just show up with more."

"Every time" !

I was so happy to have my children back, I didn't put that description together until much later. It sounded like my old schoolmate Archie. But why would Archie do all these crazy things to me? I never did anything to him, and always considered him a friend. Still, I let the authorities know, and I asked them to start seeing if they could track his were-a-bouts from the time this all started. I know it seemed far fetched, but it was our first clue in any respect. I could see him doing Ms. Grossman, that was for sure, but how could he know all my movements so well? He was very smart, and the more I thought about it, he could pull all this off.

When the detectives checked things out about Archie, he was at every place there was a murder except Peter's Murder. Peter was my daughters friend that I caught her with doing drugs. Anise said, "Look Gerald, I think this guy is involved in some way, and he has help".

"There has to be two of them working together."

"I just don't think this guy is built to do all this by himself."

"I've seen cases where there are two killers that feel the same way about there victim, and want to exact punishment together in order to get away with the act involved."

I thought about what she said and told her, "Let's see if anyone has any flights in, or out of town the same time as Archie in the past year and a half that works with me, or for me, and then we can find out if he knows anyone that is around me."

"If we can find a common denominator then we got the bastard." Heaven help who it is!"

22

CHAPTER

It took the FBI about two and half weeks to cross reference Archie's Movements along with all personnel, and friends that were associated with me. They came up with only one name for two of the days that Archie was near to me, and that was Bob. It could have been a coincidence since it was only two times, but it was a start.

They should have never told me that Bob was a suspect, because it changed the way I perceived him now. He would come into the house, "hey you guys, how are you doing today"?

"Hear anything Today about that asshole?"

I would get real short in my conversations with him.

I would answer him and say something like, "don't worry about what we heard, let the FBI take care of things".

"They are close, and when they find the bastard, there will be hell to pay."

"Now, could you excuse Anise and I, we are busy right now."

"We really don't want any company today Bob."

Bob at first would say, "okay you guys, see you later."

But after awhile he started to feel something was wrong because we were letting everyone else stay but him.

"Okay! Why is it that every time I come by lately I'm not wanted"?

"What's up?" Of course we couldn't tell him why, so things got complicated.

Anise pulled him to the side and said,

"With all Gerald is going through, you have to understand he's touchy nowadays."

Just bare with him Bob, he will come through this soon I'm sure." She was good. This is why the people that do these investigations don't let you get involved if you're too close to the case. I couldn't pretend I was alright with Bob no matter how much I tried. I was supposed to be this great actor, and couldn't hide my feelings for trying to hurt the person that hurt Katherine. So what I did was tell myself that Bob was not guilty until they had real proof. I learned a big lesson too, because the FBI ended up clearing Bob. Those two days that coincided with Archie's schedule, Bob was on a case.

I felt really foolish. Still, I didn't tell Bob why he was treated badly for that period of time, and it was a good thing I didn't.

The FBI told us that someone had used Bob's ID on those days. That he couldn't have been in two places at once. They could proof without a reasonable doubt that he was somewhere else on the days that his ID was used. That meant it was someone that was close to Bob and me. Albert!

Who else could it be? If I told Bob, he might feel the same way that I do. That Albert was the only one that could get close to him and me, and he might let on that we were back on his trail.

If Albert knew Archie, Albert could have let Archie stab Katherine. He was the only thing between the killer and Katherine. Also, Albert believed my voice was a unnatural thing after not using it for so long. He had even mentioned that he might think I made a deal with the Devil to be able to sing.

That was a sick thing to say I thought, and it is just like this maniac that's hunting me, and my family's frame of thought. We just have to find that Archie somehow knows Albert. I was confused with who I could trust, and not trust around me. Everyone in my mind was a suspect now. I needed to talk to someone besides Anise, and I did't know what to do about that.

So I decided to call Mr. TD Jakes and see if I could get some spiritual guidance because my heart was turning hateful towards Albert and Archie, and the want I had in me to take their lives if they were guilty, was tearing me apart inside. I couldn't sleep. I tossed and turned all night, waiting for some proof. In my mind they were already guilty. I could feel it inside. The hate was eating me inside and I didn't want to feel like that. I wanted to be like other people I had heard about in my life and be able to show some kind of forgiveness, but I just couldn't find that path. So I had my people call his people, and arrange to see if I could come back and see him again.

I really respected Mr. Jakes and really wanted to hear what advice he would have for my situation. I was sure he had never had anyone come to him with problems like mine. With a killer threatening to kill me, and my family, and even friends. He had read in the newspapers about Katherine and I filled him in on the rest. He leaned back in his big leather chair in contemplation of what he was going to say to me. After a while he spoke.

He said, "GeraldWhen your people called me, I knew your spirit was troubled."

"I mean, you are going through something that many people can't even imagine."

"The lost of loved ones through violence, being stalked by a crazed killer, or two, is something that I've never had to deal with."

"I don't know anybody that has, and don't want to ever experience what you're going through."

"But there is someone that has been through everything, and that is God." "King David had enemies like you even though he was a good man."

"He made mistakes like you, and lived in pressure from his surroundings."

"But, David prayed all the time, and asked God all the time, what move Should I make next Lord?

"The times he didn't ask for God's help, things didn't work out too good for him".

"In this matter you cannot in no way depend on your own understanding."

"In the Bible, are many stories of death, deception, and murder, through lust, jealousy, greed and many other reasons."

"Pray my son, and God will guide you in your directions, and decisions in this matter."

"Only he can show you what moves to make. I sure can't, and no man can."

"This is where man needs God's understanding."

"If you Pray on it, trust in God, He will answer your Prayers in this matter, because you're a good man," "and because you have no one else to turn to in a situation like this".

"He may not answer the way you would like, or in the time you would like, but he will answer".

"Wait on the Lord".

I think he knew I was going to try and kill this person or persons when I caught them, and he was trying to tell me also that God would fight this battle, and to not be like them and take things in my own hands. That is why God made laws. I got the message. Let God !

Mr. Jakes had a way of giving you hope, and courage, in times of need, and I was so glad I came to him. He was right of course. Only God could help me through this. I didn't want to become a killer myself. That was weighing on the back of my mind without even realizing it. I wanted to kill this person or persons. I didn't want a trial. I didn't want any chance of them getting off.

Without even committing the act of murder, I had become like them. I was planning to kill.

I returned home to L.A. and Anise, just to find Iturbi waiting for me at the house. He had this disturbing look on his face, and was dying to tell me the reason for this look.

He asked me,to sit before he started talking. He said, "Gerald I believe it's Albert, and your old school mate Archie that is doing this to you."

"I crossed referenced the times they traveled, and in that cross I found they know each other." "They knew each other for about ten years before your career took off.

Archie has known about you for years and never got in touch with you for whatever reason. He knew Albert and kept up on you, but it wasn't until your singing started that they started really talking. Then the phone calls stopped. I figure they must be contacting each other in a different way so that they couldn't be traced if they were suspected. I think they think you are evil. They belong to this cult that believes that they are here to help God rid the world of the devils deciples. Anise told me, "Fuck what this is about, people are dead!

"We are gonna bait these bastards in and either bust them or kill them."

"So let's get busy with a plan." This woman was really growing on me. I said, "I like your way of thinking young lady, let's get down."

23

CHAPTER

We didn't tell anyone what we were planning just in case we had to kill them ourselves. I didn't feel the same way about that since I talked to Mr. Jakes, but Anise and I were leaving the door open just in case things didn't work out the way we wanted them to. So we came up with a plan, and began to put it in fruition.

I had a play coming up, and I was to start rehearsals in two weeks so we had time to prepare our trap. The theater was the Pasadena Playhouse, and it was perfect for what we had in store for whomever showed up. I asked the owner to install some hidden cameras at my expense, and to keep it to himself what they were for because, I was trying to surprise some big wigs at Sony that were coming to see the show. I told him that only the people installing the camera's could know about the camera's. When they were done putting up the camera's, you couldn't even see a hole in the wall. It was perfect!

Four days before the play was to start, I announced that the first show was to be for the poor that couldn't afford a ticket. I held a lottery at most of the Radio Stations in the area, and sent them hundreds of tickets. I gave ten tickets to each of the people that worked for me, and made sure they understood that there were no numbered seats. It was first come, first serve. This way they knew there was no way to trace the seating of the ticket holder. The camera's would show me where people were sitting, and who they were. I told everyone that was involved with security, that This performance didn't need any this night because this was for the poor, and that they didn't need police around them. They had enough of that in their everyday lives, and didn't need anymore problems. I wanted them to enjoy the show. I knew this would bait these murdering bastards. I felt bad about using the poor people in this matter, but this was life. and death, and I knew if any group of people could handle this kind of thing it would be the poor people that went through this kind of stuff a lot in their lives. I might even get some backup from some of them.

Rich folks would run to save their ass, poor people might run,but they are going to look at what's happening while they are running. That's for sure.

Albert, and Bob, came to me and told me I was crazy to not have security. Albert said, "Your really asking for it man." "What the hell are you thinking"? I assured him that the person involved would not dare to try anything at this time. They would be thinking that there would be security, and wouldn't dare to try anything. Albert, and Bob, knew that no matter what I asked the FBI that they would still have someone following me around. At least outside the theater. So Albert knew he would still have to be careful. Anise didn't know Archie, but was on the lookout for him.

She had a photo, and as an Ex-FBI agent, she was more than equipped to handle the situation. No one knew about her ability to fight but me. If Albert, or anyone came at her, I knew she could handle herself. I had sparred with Albert, and Anise was a much more formidable opponent. I didn't like her being in harm's way. I felt like she was trying to be bait for the killers. She had done this kind of stuff before in the line of duty and had to kill someone to protect herself. She had also beat some assailants damn near to death a couple of times so I knew she had experience and wouldn't panic. She was so hard headed in this matter.

I couldn't talk her into staying out of the way. The truth of the matter was, I only trusted her, and no one else. Her love for me, and her ability, and experience in fighting, was part of my strength in this thing, and we did plan this trap together, still, I had to worry about her. I already lost one love. I couldn't live with another loss of that magnitude.

The night of the show had come, and there was a strange feeling in the air I couldn't explain. I was leaving myself open on purpose to draw out the killers but that Isn't what was making me feel funny. It was like a feeling of impending doom, like the end of the world or something.

I suddenly don't feel confident with the plan Anise and I had come up with, but it was too late.

The machinery was in motion. All things were in place, and despite the feeling I had, everything was going according to plan. Although Anise and I were also carrying 9mm weapons as back up, I felt that Anise being involved wasn't cool now despite her training. I was in love again, and couldn't stand to lose her too. As the start time to the show drew nearer, I felt less and less confident in letting her be involved. She was being bait also by being there, no matter how you look at it. The plan sounded great when we came up with it, now I couldn't believe I'd let someone I love do this with me. What the hell was I thinking?

Albert had come to the theater about a half hour before the show just like many other people that came to see the show. Nothing seemed out of the ordinary with his actions. Anise was following him as best she could through the crowd. He got a program, and got a seat as close to the stage as he could. I don't see how he was going to try anything tonight. He would have to be crazy. He could never get away with harming me or Anise with such a big crowd around.

The children were at home and protected by the watchful eye of the FBI. They were around the theater too regardless of my request as expected, and I was sure they had someone in the audience as well. Once the show was to start, I wasn't supposed to make an entrance until almost the end of the first act. All of the theater workers, and actors, will be watching from behind the curtain, or working the lights, and props, to make the show work.

Albert knew that, and this would be a good time to try something. Later in the play, I would be on stage by myself for almost the whole act four, but he would have to do something to me in front of all those folks. Archie wasn't the physical type so he would have to sneak up on someone to do some harm. Archie wasn't at the theater, but I had Iturbi on him. Last we heard from Iturbi was that Archie was heading in the direction of the theater. These two had only been around me at the same time according to the records, once, that was the night that Katherine was killed.

I really felt that if Archie showed up, that they were going to try something and I would kill them both. I was imagining how I would do them both when I got a knock on my dressing room door. I cautiously moved towards the door and spoke as loud as I could.

"Who is it"? "Iturbi Gerald, Open the door". Iturbi was all excited as he spoke.

"I followed Archie straight here from the airport. He didn't make any stops anywhere. He came right here.

I don't know how, but they are gonna try something tonight."

I was ready for everything, or so I thought.

The show was going great, and the crowd was loving what they were seeing and hearing. After the intermission, I started the play off. Everyone had went and had their refreshments and was settled down. I had a big song by myself on stage and was rocking the crowd when all of a sudden I felt a burning sensation in my shoulder. I grabbed my left shoulder, and saw that I was bleeding. I had been shot.

I passed out on the stage. Anise jumped up on the stage from out of the audience, and started yelling for help. Iturbi got on the radio and called for backup. The crowd started running out of the theater, people were being stepped on, but not that many people got hurt thank God.

I woke up in the hospital with a bullet hole in my shoulder and was confused. I asked if Anise was alright cause I had passed out. Once I saw her come in the room I asked for the surveillance footage. Surveillance showed a rifle barrel coming from the rafters with no image of the shooter. Albert and Archie's whereabouts were accounted for. What the hell is going on I thought. When is this nightmare going to end? I know that Archie and Albert are involved.

Anise says, "there has to be a third party," I said, "What the fuck!
"Are you trying to tell me that There are a whole bunch of people that
want to kill me that badly."

"What the hell have I done to deserve some shit like this:?"

Anise walked towards me and put my arms around her waist, then
she put hers around me and said, "calm down baby, we will get these
mother-fuckers, I promise."

"We have the right people, they just have someone else working with
them that we missed".

"There are three instead of two."

"Just as she said that I thought about Susan".

If Archie and Susan were Still married, she was crazy enough to
follow Archie through anything".

"She loved the ground he walked on".

I wouldn't be able to fight the way I wanted to now with this hole in
my shoulder for at least a couple of months, and they were getting des-
perate now. They shot me. I had to make some kind of aggressive move,
regardless of my condition. I told Anise I needed to get Archie alone so
l could have a chat with him.

I couldn't check out the hospital for a couple of days so they could
make sure I had no infections from the bullet. So we waited a week.
The show had to be called off because my shows had become dangerous to my fans. We refunded the ticket money, and my career was put
on hold.

The news wanted to know if we had any ideas, or clues, as to the
whereabouts of who shot me.

We lied and said no. The news people were really cruel with the po-
lice and FBI by this time. They put every detail in the news about what
I've been through. The loss of my wife, even down to Ms. Grossman.
That's when we got the next letter.

"You'll never do another show, devil." That was all the letter said.

Anise and I stayed in the house for almost a month just having food
brought in with no visitors but the children. I didn't see any friends. I
wanted the killers to think they had won. Once everyone got a little laid

back, I snuck out the house. Anise acted like I was still in the house by answering all calls, and the door, when the police did their hourly check. I de-guised myself with a fake beard, and wore a little body make-up to make myself look fatter.

Anise used her connections to get me a fake California Identification Card so I wouldn't have any problem at the airport. I was on my way to see Archie, and beat some answers out his ass.

Archie lived in a nice high rise apartment in Riverdale, New York in the Bronx. It was a quiet neighborhood, with a mostly Jewish content of people living in the area. At night time, people were usually home and getting ready for the next day's work, so movement was scarce. I hoped that Archie would be a night dweller since he was into killing like any other murderer, sneaking around at night, to do his dirty work, and not be seen by the neighborhood residents. I was right. I didn't have to wait long at all. I arrived in his neighborhood around nine o'clock, and sat across the street in a rented car and waited. By ten o'clock, he was coming out of his building heading for his car. I rolled up on him. He tried to run when he spotted me, but he was to fat and out of shape to get any distance between me and him. I hit him in the back of his head with a back hand that jarred him into unconsciousness.

I drove my car over to him I opened the trunk, picked him up, and threw him inside. I drove down the West Side Highway to the 125th exit. It was dark, and quiet there. The only Problem was that it was wide open. It was near the water with no building to block what I wanted to do to him whatever that was.

There was a gas station a little way up the street, and the famous Cotton Club was across the street from the gas station but it was closed. The jury was still out on killing him. I didn't want to be like him, but he killed my wife. I was confused as to my missions end. I was sure of one thing though, I was going to beat him senseless. I figured I'd use my money, and fame to beat anything that happened in court later.

As soon as I open the trunk and pull him out, a car pulls up but no one gets out. Sometimes people park over here near the water and make love in their cars late at night and I had forgotten about that. Most people mind their business in New York so I kept to my course and took the chance that whomever was in the car was that type, that didn't see anything.

My intentions was to beat this asshole into some answers, then whatever happened after that happened. First punch was to the stomach, then to the chest just hard enough to let him know that there was more to come and that this was going to be a long night for him. My first question, "Why Katherine"? "Why didn't you just come after me?

"She was a beautiful spirit that never hurt a fly. Why"? He looked at me and laughed. I hit him so hard with a back hand that it dropped him to his knees.

When he got up I said, "You want some more you son of a bitch."

Then I hit him in the stomach again. Archie just smiled with this sick look on his face and said, "You always had everything didn't you Gerald".

"You always thought you were the shit."

I said, "what the fuck are you talking about asshole, I never bothered you in my life you sick faggot."

He said, "I was the best singer in the school until you came."

"Everything was so easy for you." "I worked and worked to keep my voice right".

"You just wait twenty five years and decide to sing perfectly."

"No practice for years."

"No time taken to nurture your talent," "just awaken it when you want to and expect people to not think that you're not evil".

I said to Archie, "You should hear how retarded you sound." Your a fucking maniac who killed innocent people because you think my talent is from hell."

"Why didn't you just come after me and no one else."

Archie replied, "Because you had instruments that were assigned to help you to this point in your life."

"It's the devils design you have lived by and all that have helped along the way will perish along with you".

"Archie, you are some sick fuck".

"I didn't know that you were this fucked up."

I started beating the crap out of him and asking him, "where was Susan and Albert".

"He looked surprised when I said Albert". I grabbed his Adam's Apple and started choking him, I said to him as he gasped for air, "what is Albert getting ready to do"? "What was that look for"? He tried to say something, but I was choking him too hard. I let my fingers loosened a little, so he could speak.

He said, "it's too late for us and you."

"We knew you would come to me first." "Bob is on our side, not Albert you idiot".

"Bob used false ID, and a fake beard, to disguise himself as Albert."

"Your woman Anise will meet you hell tonight."

Just then I felt something whisk by my head. It was a bullet that just missed my head. I grabbed Archie, and put him in front of me in the direction of the bullet.

I was at 125th street near the water on the west side, and there wasn't anywhere to hide but behind the car. I could see clearly that it was Susan firing a handgun at me as she walked closer. These two were ready to die tonight. They were willing to give up their lives for this belief that I was evil. What sick mother fuckers they had become.

He started talking shit as I held him in front of me. "You're not too smart are you Gerald"?

"We knew that you would come for us one night, so Susan always leaves the house right after me to watch my back since she's the better marksman".

"You can't get away". "Sorry she missed you on stage".

She just kept walking towards me with the gun pointed right at me. She was looking for a good shot but the darkness of night was obscuring her vision, and I knew she didn't want to hit Archie. I kept him close, but I couldn't do it for long. I was going to have to make a run for it.

Then there was a pop. Susan went down. Someone came towards us with a gun in hand. I didn't recognize who it was until he got close to me and spoke. I knew that voice, It was Albert, and he was beardless.

Albert said, "I figured I would follow you for a while, and give you some back up."

"I sat right behind you on the plane and you didn't even recognize me."

"You looked so stupid with that fake ass beard, and bodysuit."

I said, "I've never seen you without your beard."

"You look like a human." I could hear sirens coming our way in the distance.

Albert said, 'I took the liberty of calling the police beforeI shot this young lady".

Susan lay there bleeding from the upper thigh and in very serious pain.

Archie was just lost. He fell to the ground like his legs had fallen out from under him. I called Anise to let her know what was going on, but I only kept getting her voice mail.

Back in LA, Bob thought he had Anise all to himself to kill. The surprise was about to be on him. He made a prank call to the FBI to inform them that someone saw me at the airport boarding a plane. The agents outside my house came to the door and asked Anise could they speak to me personally. She informed them that I must have sneaked out while she was asleep.

Of course they didn't believe she didn't know I was gone, and all of them left to go back to their main office and try to figure out where I was. They were not assigned to watch her, and she wasn't family to me. They also figured she could take care of herself being an Ex-FBI. Their concern was to locate me. Bob knew that.

Anise went back to the bedroom to prepare to relax, and watch television. She was concerned about me and what I was up to, but couldn't do anything but wait on my call.

She felt secure in the house at this time since Archie and his Wife were in New York three thousand miles away. Albert was in LA she thought but he wouldn't try anything while she was locked in the house. Still, to feel even safer, she put on her favorite workout Danskin tights just in case she had to move fast for any reason. She was ready for anything and was hoping in a way that Albert would come there and try something thinking she was alone and helpless.

A couple of hours went by and still no phone call from me. That isn't what we agreed on. I was supposed to check in every couple of hours. She didn't want to call me because she didn't know if the ringing of the phone would compromise whatever I was doing. But, she was getting worried for me and needed to hear from me. She remembered she could text me because his text messages were on vibrate. She texted me and just said, "call me asap."

She picked up the house phone to make sure it was working and to her surprise it wasn't.

As she put the phone down, the doorbell rang. She went to the front door to see who it was. "Who's there?: "It's Bob Anise, let me in". She opened the door right away feeling a sense of gladness that Bob showed up when he did. She felt safety in numbers and with Bob there Albert didn't have a chance. Bob came in and had his acting face on of concern, and confusion, as to why there were no guards outside. Anise told him what took place, and Bob assured her that he would stay with her until she heard from me knowing all along that he was the one that made that crank call to the FBI. Anise said to Bob, would you like a drink",

"I sure could use one".

He replied, "thanks, scotch and soda." She had to go to the bar to fix the drink, he followed behind her, and grabbed her from behind by the neck. There were no words said. Anise was surprised, but not unprepared. She was always on ready mode. She grabbed his fingers in a twisting motion that made Bob's body contort in the direction she chose to send him.

He went crashing to his knees. Anise lost hold of his hand, and he regrouped and went to attack her.

As he approached her he said, 'you've been practicing huh"?

Anise responded "yes all my life bitch."

She kicked him in the chest, and rolled around in the same motion and swept his feet from under him. He fell onto the floor near the bar. He rolled away from her so he could get to his feet and began his attack.

He threw punches, and kicks, most being repelled by Anise's defense. He got in a backhand to the side of her head, but paid for that with a tiger claw to the face that took off half the skin off his face.

Bob was in shock. This woman was a beast and the more punishment he took, the more he thought this woman was working for Satan too. He couldn't beat her, so he went for his gun.

That was the last move he ever made. Instinct took over Anise and she gave Bob a kick to the throat that brought his Adams Apple to the back of his neck. He gasped for air but to no avail. He fell to his knees and choked to death from the blow right on the living room floor. Anise knew right away that he had to be down with Archie and Susan. She got on the cell phone and called me to warn me.

When I answered the phone, I was so glad to know that Anise was alright. I explained what had happened to me in New York, she then called the FBI and let them know what had happened.

First, Anise and I had to deal with the police in two different cities before being reunited. I told Anise, "I am so glad you handled yourself so well, and I'm proud of you".

"I thank God Everything is alright."

24

CHAPTER

The case was all wrapped up now. It ends up that Bob, Archie and Susan had met at a religious meeting they had gone to way before I started singing., I guess they never read the Bible. God Doesn't like murderers. Their sick minds let them believe they were doing the right thing. God fights the battles of those that believe in him. These three just used this cult as an excuse to kill and exact punishment on those that they were jealous of. All three of them had issues of jealousy.

Archie and Susan had always had jealousy issues and Bob became jealous when he heard me sing for the first time. There are always people that hate when someone is doing good. He had been at a seminar with Archie and Susan and they saw me on TV at the bar of the hotel they were staying at.

Bob said, "I worked with that guy for years and he never sang a note'.

"Who would have known."

Archie and Susan said, "we went to school with him. They told Bob the whole story and said that it was impossible to sing that good without practicing.

They told him I had an evil presence in school and that I had to be stopped. That is when they got together and planned this scheme to get rid of me and my loved ones. Even friends. That was just sickness on their parts. When I was told why all this murder and hate had happened to me, I felt sadness and pity for Archie and Susan and Bob. They were really sick! I lost all my hate for them and felt I had to pray for them.

It was strange. I wanted to pray for the people that killed my wife. I wanted to forgive them.

Maybe with time, but I wasn't ready yet. I still had a part of me that thought they shouldn't be living in this world. Katherine had so much to live for. All those years in school, and raising the children with me, gone. It wasn't fair. Them getting life in prison, or the death penalty still wouldn't bring her back, or anyone else they murdered. There was no punishment in my eyes that was equal to what they had done. So I had to belief that God would take care of this for me along with man's law.

As time went by, and My marriage to Anise was prospering fully. The children had straightened up their lives, and were working as my personal assistant's. They kept all my business activities in line, as well as time tables and my Intel stock as well as other investments.

They became my right and left hand. I couldn't have asked for better assistants. Archie, Susan, were sentenced to life in prison in New York, but had to answer for their crimes in California and Atlanta. California gave them the death penalty.

I dedicated my life to Christ and My wife did also, and I sang mostly for Mr T.D. Jakes church on Sunday's even though his church was in Texas. We bought a house in Dallas Texas so we could be comfortable, when we flew down on the weekends, but we still stayed at the house in L.A. most of the time.

My life had become a very happy and full filled one after all that happened. Everything being in it's place as it should be in the eyes of a happy, successful man and yet there still seemed to be something is missing. I seemed to be spread out in all I was. I was a singer, actor, martial artist, father and husband, but I was all these things as a separate entity. The man needed to be all these things together as a whole. I determined it was my spirituality that was needed to make me whole. I had to get right with God and did. Once I did that My Life was complete.

Looking back on my life now I realize that everything that has happened in my life is by Gods Design. We do have free will to make the choices we make in life but in the end What is Meant to Be is Meant to be............

Printed in the United States
by Baker & Taylor Publisher Services

Printed in the United States
by Baker & Taylor Publisher Services